The House at Pooh Corner

A.A.Milne

with decorations by
E.H.Shepard

EGMONT

DEDICATION

You gave me Christopher Robin, and then
You breathed new life in Pooh.
Whatever of each has left my pen
Goes homing back to you.
My book is ready, and comes to greet
The mother it longs to see –
It would be my present to you, my sweet,
If it weren't your gift to me.

CONTRADICTION

An Introduction is to introduce people, but Christopher Robin and his friends, who have already been introduced to you, are now going to say Good-bye. So this is the opposite. When we asked Pooh what the opposite of an Introduction was he said, 'The what of a what?' which didn't help us as much as we had hoped, but luckily Owl kept his head and told us that the Opposite of an Introduction, my dear Pooh, was a Contradiction; and, as he is very good at long words, I am sure that that's what it is.

Why we are having a Contradiction is because last week when Christopher Robin said to me, 'What about that story you were going to tell me about what happened to Pooh when —' I happened to say very quickly, 'What about nine times a hundred and seven?' And when we had done that one, we had one about cows going through a gate at two a minute, and there are three hundred in the field, so how many are left after an hour and a half? We find these very exciting, and when we have been excited quite enough, we curl up and go to sleep . . . and Pooh, sitting wakeful a little longer on his chair by our pillow, thinks Grand Thoughts

to himself about Nothing, until he, too, closes his eyes and nods his head, and follows us on tiptoe into the Forest. There, still, we have magic adventures, more wonderful than any I have told you about; but now, when we wake up in the morning, they are gone before we can catch hold of them. How did the last one begin? 'One day when Pooh was walking in the Forest, there were one hundred and seven cows on a gate . . .' No, you see, we have lost it. It was the best, I think. Well, here are some of the other ones, all that we shall remember now. But, of course it isn't really Good-bye, because the Forest will always be there . . . and anybody who is Friendly with Bears can find it.

A.A.M.

CONTENTS

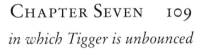

CHAPTER ONE

in which a house is built at
Pooh Corner for Eeyore

ONE DAY when Pooh Bear had nothing else to do, he thought he would do something, so he went round to Piglet's house to see what Piglet was doing. It was still snowing as he stumped over the white forest track, and he expected to find Piglet warming his toes in front of his fire, but to his surprise he saw that the door was open, and the more he looked inside the more Piglet wasn't there.

'He's out,' said Pooh sadly. 'That's what it is. He's not in. I shall have to go a fast Thinking Walk by myself. Bother!'

But first he thought that he would knock very loudly just to make *quite* sure . . . and while he waited for Piglet not to answer, he jumped up and down to keep warm, and a hum came suddenly into his head, which seemed to him a Good Hum, such as is Hummed Hopefully to Others.

The more it snows
  (Tiddely pom),
The more it goes
  (Tiddely pom),
The more it goes
  (Tiddely pom),
On snowing.
And nobody knows
  (Tiddely pom),
How cold my toes
  (Tiddely pom),
How cold my toes
  (Tiddely pom),
Are growing.

'So what I'll do,' said Pooh, 'is I'll do this. I'll just go home first and see what the time is, and perhaps I'll put a muffler round my neck, and then I'll go and see Eeyore and sing it to him.'

He hurried back to his own house; and his mind was so busy on the way with the hum that he was getting ready for Eeyore that, when he suddenly saw Piglet sitting in his best arm-chair, he could only stand there rubbing his head and wondering whose house he was in.

'Hallo, Piglet,' he said. 'I thought you were out.'

'No,' said Piglet, 'it's you who were out, Pooh.'

'So it was,' said Pooh. 'I knew one of us was.'

He looked up at his clock, which had stopped at five minutes to eleven some weeks ago.

'Nearly eleven o'clock,' said Pooh happily. 'You're just in time for a little smackerel of something,' and he put his head into the cupboard. 'And then we'll go out, Piglet, and sing my song to Eeyore.'

'Which song, Pooh?'

'The one we're going to sing to Eeyore,' explained Pooh.

The clock was still saying five minutes to eleven when Pooh and Piglet set out on their way half an hour later. The wind had dropped, and the snow, tired of rushing round in circles trying to catch itself up, now fluttered gently down until it found a place on which to rest, and sometimes the place was Pooh's nose and sometimes it wasn't, and in a little while Piglet was wearing a white muffler round his neck and feeling more snowy behind the ears than he had ever felt before.

'Pooh,' he said at last, and a little timidly, because he didn't want Pooh to think he was Giving In, 'I was just wondering. How would it be if we went home now and *practised* your song, and then sang it to Eeyore tomorrow – or – or the next day, when we happen to see him?'

'That's a very good idea, Piglet,' said Pooh. 'We'll practise it now as we go along. But it's no good going home to practise it, because it's a special Outdoor Song which Has To Be Sung In The Snow.'

'Are you sure?' asked Piglet anxiously.

'Well, you'll see, Piglet, when you listen. Because this is how it begins. *The more it snows, tiddely pom –*'

'Tiddely what?' said Piglet.

'Pom,' said Pooh. 'I put that in to make it more hummy. *The more it goes, tiddely pom, the more –*

'Didn't you say snows?'

'Yes, but that was *before.*'

'Before the tiddely pom?'

'It was a *different* tiddely pom,' said Pooh, feeling rather muddled now. 'I'll sing it to you properly and then you'll see.'

So he sang it again.

The more it
SNOWS-tiddely-pom
The more it
GOES-tiddely-pom
The more it
GOES-tiddely-pom
On
Snowing.
And nobody
KNOWS-tiddely-pom,
How cold my
TOES-tiddely-pom
How cold my
TOES-tiddely-pom
Are
Growing.

He sang it like that, which is much the best way of singing it, and when he had finished, he waited for Piglet to say that, of all the Outdoor Hums for Snowy Weather he had ever heard, this was the best. And, after thinking the matter out carefully, Piglet said:

'Pooh,' he said solemnly, 'it isn't the *toes* so much as the *ears*.'

By this time they were getting near Eeyore's Gloomy Place, which was where he lived, and as it was still very snowy behind Piglet's ears, and he was getting tired of it, they turned into a little pine-wood, and sat down on the gate which led into it. They were out of the snow now, but it was very cold, and to keep themselves warm they sang Pooh's song right through six times, Piglet doing the tiddely-poms and Pooh doing the rest of it, and both of them thumping on the top of the gate with pieces of stick at the proper places. And in a little while they felt much warmer, and were able to talk again.

'I've been thinking,' said Pooh, 'and what I've been thinking about is this. I've been thinking about Eeyore.'

'What about Eeyore?'

'Well, poor Eeyore has nowhere to live.'

'Nor he has,' said Piglet.

'*You* have a house, Piglet, and I have a house, and they are very good houses. And Christopher Robin has a house, and Owl and Kanga and Rabbit have houses, and even Rabbit's friends and relations have houses or somethings, but poor Eeyore has nothing. So what I've been thinking is: Let's build him a house.'

'That,' said Piglet, 'is a Grand Idea. Where shall we build it?'

'We will build it here,' said Pooh, 'just by this wood, out of the wind, because this is where I thought of it. And we will call this Pooh Corner. And we will build an Eeyore House with sticks at Pooh Corner for Eeyore.'

'There was a heap of sticks on the other side of the wood,' said Piglet. 'I saw them. Lots and lots. All piled up.'

'Thank you, Piglet,' said Pooh. 'What you have just said will be a Great Help to us, and because of it I could call this place Poohanpiglet Corner if Pooh Corner didn't sound better, which it does, being smaller and more like a corner. Come along.'

So they got down off the gate and went round to the other side of the wood to fetch the sticks.

*　*　*

Christopher Robin had spent the morning indoors going to Africa and back, and he had just got off the boat and was wondering what it was like outside, when who

should come knocking at the door but Eeyore.

'Hallo, Eeyore,' said Christopher Robin, as he opened the door and came out. 'How are you?'

'It's snowing still,' said Eeyore gloomily.

'So it is.'

'*And* freezing.'

'Is it?'

'Yes,' said Eeyore. 'However,' he said, brightening up a little, 'we haven't had an earthquake lately.'

'What's the matter, Eeyore?'

'Nothing, Christopher Robin. Nothing important.

I suppose you haven't seen a house or what-not anywhere about?'

'What sort of a house?'

'Just a house.'

'Who lives there?'

'I do. At least I thought I did. But I suppose I don't. After all, we can't all have houses.'

'But, Eeyore, I didn't know – I always thought –'

'I don't know how it is, Christopher Robin, but what with all this snow and one thing and another, not to mention icicles and such-like, it isn't so Hot in my field about three o'clock in the morning as some people think it is. It isn't Close, if you know what I mean – not so as to be uncomfortable. It isn't Stuffy. In fact, Christopher Robin,' he went on in a loud whisper, 'quite-between-ourselves-and-don't-tell-anybody, it's Cold.'

'Oh, Eeyore!'

'And I said to myself: The others will be sorry if I'm getting myself all cold. They haven't got Brains, any of them, only grey fluff that's blown into their heads by mistake, and they don't Think, but if it goes on snowing for another six weeks or so, one of them will begin to say to himself: "Eeyore can't be so very much too Hot about three o'clock in the morning." And then it will Get About. And they'll be Sorry.'

'Oh, Eeyore!' said Christopher Robin, feeling very sorry already.

'I don't mean you, Christopher Robin. You're different. So what it all comes to is that I built myself a house down by my little wood.'

'Did you really? How exciting!'

'The really exciting part,' said Eeyore in his most melancholy voice, 'is that when I left it this morning it was there, and when I came back it wasn't. Not at all, very natural, and it was only Eeyore's house. But still I just wondered.'

Christopher Robin didn't stop to wonder. He was already back in *his* house, putting on his waterproof hat, his waterproof boots, and his waterproof macintosh as fast as he could.

'We'll go and look for it at once,' he called out to Eeyore.

'Sometimes,' said Eeyore, 'when people have quite finished taking a person's house, there are one or two bits which they don't want and are rather glad for the person to take back, if you know what I mean. So I thought if we just went –'

'Come on,' said Christopher Robin, and off they hurried, and in a very little time they got to the corner of the field by the side of the pine-wood, where Eeyore's house wasn't any longer.

'There!' said Eeyore. 'Not a stick of it left! Of course, I've still got all this snow to do what I like with. One mustn't complain.'

But Christopher Robin wasn't listening to Eeyore, he was listening to something else.

'Can you hear it?' he asked.

'What is it? Somebody laughing?'

'Listen.'

They both listened . . . and they heard a deep gruff voice saying in a singing voice that the more it snowed the more it went on snowing, and a small high voice tiddely-pomming in between.

'It's Pooh,' said Christopher Robin excitedly . . .

'Possibly,' said Eeyore.

'*And* Piglet!' said Christopher Robin excitedly.

'Probably,' said Eeyore. 'What we want is a Trained Bloodhound.'

The words of the song changed suddenly.

'*We've finished our HOUSE!*' sang the gruff voice.

'*Tiddely pom!*' sang the squeaky one.

'*It's a beautiful HOUSE . . .*'

'*Tiddely pom . . .*'

'*I wish it were MINE . . .*'

'*Tiddely pom . . .*'

'Pooh!' shouted Christopher Robin . . .

The singers on the gate stopped suddenly.

'It's Christopher Robin!' said Pooh eagerly.

'He's round by the place where we got all those sticks from,' said Piglet.

'Come on,' said Pooh.

They climbed down their gate and hurried round the corner of the wood, Pooh making welcoming noises all the way.

'Why, here *is* Eeyore,' said Pooh, when he had finished hugging Christopher Robin, and he nudged Piglet, and Piglet nudged him, and they thought to themselves what a lovely surprise they had got ready. 'Hallo, Eeyore.'

'Same to you, Pooh Bear, and twice on Thursdays,' said Eeyore gloomily.

Before Pooh could say: 'Why Thursdays?' Christopher Robin began to explain the sad story of Eeyore's Lost House. And Pooh and Piglet listened, and their eyes seemed to get bigger and bigger.

'*Where* did you say it was?' asked Pooh.

'Just here,' said Eeyore.

'Made of sticks?'

'Yes.'

'Oh!' said Piglet.

'What?' said Eeyore.

'I just said "Oh!"' said Piglet nervously. And so as to seem quite at ease he hummed tiddely-pom once or twice in a what-shall-we-do-now kind of way.

'You're sure it *was* a house?' said Pooh. 'I mean, you're sure the house was just here?'

'Of course I am,' said Eeyore. And he murmured to himself, 'No brain at all, some of them.'

'Why, what's the matter, Pooh?' asked Christopher Robin.

'Well,' said Pooh . . . 'The fact *is*,' said Pooh . . . 'Well, the fact *is*,' said Pooh . . . 'You see,' said Pooh . . . 'It's like this,' said Pooh, and something seemed to tell him that he wasn't explaining very well, and he nudged Piglet again.

'It's like this,' said Piglet quickly . . . 'Only warmer,' he added after deep thought.

'What's warmer?'

'The other side of the wood, where Eeyore's house is.'

'*My* house?' said Eeyore. 'My house was here.'

'No,' said Piglet firmly. 'The other side of the wood.'

'Because of being warmer,' said Pooh.

'But I ought to *know* –'

'Come and look,' said Piglet simply, and he led the way.

'There wouldn't be *two* houses,' said Pooh. 'Not so close together.'

They came round the corner, and there was Eeyore's house, looking as comfy as anything.

'There you are,' said Piglet.

'Inside as well as outside,' said Pooh proudly.

Eeyore went inside . . . and came out again.

'It's a remarkable thing,' he said. 'It *is* my house, and I built it where I said I did, so the wind must have blown it here. And the wind blew it right over the wood, and blew it down here, and here it is as good as ever. In fact, better in places.'

'Much better,' said Pooh and Piglet together.

'It just shows what can be done by taking a little trouble,' said Eeyore. 'Do you see, Pooh? Do you see, Piglet? Brains first and then Hard Work. Look at it! *That's* the way to build a house,' said Eeyore proudly.

* * *

So they left him in it; and Christopher Robin went back to lunch with his friends Pooh and Piglet, and on the way they told him of the Awful Mistake they had made. And when he had finished laughing, they all sang the Outdoor Song for Snowy Weather the rest of the way home, Piglet, who was still not quite sure of his voice, putting in the tiddely-poms again.

'And I know it *seems* easy,' said Piglet to himself, 'but it isn't *every one* who could do it.'

CHAPTER TWO

*in which Tigger comes to
the Forest and has breakfast*

WINNIE-THE-POOH woke up suddenly in the middle of the night and listened. Then he got out of bed, and lit his candle, and stumped across the room to see if anybody was trying to get into his honey-cupboard, and they weren't, so he stumped back again, blew out his candle, and got into bed. Then he heard the noise again.

'Is that you, Piglet?' he said.

But it wasn't.

'Come in, Christopher Robin,' he said.

But Christopher Robin didn't.

'Tell me about it tomorrow, Eeyore,' said Pooh sleepily.

But the noise went on.

'*Worraworraworraworraworra*,' said Whatever-it-was, and Pooh found that he wasn't asleep after all.

'What can it be?' he thought. 'There are lots of noises in the Forest, but this is a different one. It isn't a growl, and it isn't a purr, and it isn't a bark, and it isn't the noise-you-make-before-beginning-a-piece-of-poetry, but it's a noise of some kind, made by a strange animal! And he's making it outside my door. So I shall get up and ask him not to do it.'

He got out of bed and opened his front door.

'Hallo!' said Pooh, in case there was anything outside.

'Hallo!' said Whatever-it-was.

'Oh!' said Pooh. 'Hallo!'

'Hallo!'

'Oh, *there* you are!' said Pooh. 'Hallo!'

'Hallo!' said the Strange Animal, wondering how long this was going on.

Pooh was just going to say 'Hallo!' for the fourth time when he thought that he wouldn't, so he said, 'Who is it?' instead.

'Me,' said a voice.

'Oh!' said Pooh. 'Well, come here.'

So Whatever-it-was came here, and in the light of the candle he and Pooh looked at each other.

'I'm Pooh,' said Pooh.

'I'm Tigger,' said Tigger.

'Oh!' said Pooh, for he had never seen an animal like this before. 'Does Christopher Robin know about you?'

'Of course he does,' said Tigger.

'Well,' said Pooh, 'it's the middle of the night, which is a good time for going to sleep. And to-morrow morning we'll have some honey for breakfast. Do Tiggers like honey?'

'They like everything,' said Tigger cheerfully.

'Then if they like going to sleep on the floor, I'll go back to bed,' said Pooh, 'and we'll do things in the morning. Good night.' And he got back into bed and went fast asleep.

When he awoke in the morning, the first thing he saw was Tigger, sitting in front of the glass and looking at himself.

'Hallo!' said Pooh.

'Hallo!' said Tigger. 'I've found somebody just like me. I thought I was the only one of them.'

Pooh got out of bed, and began to explain what a looking-glass was, but just as he was getting to the interesting part, Tigger said:

'Excuse me a moment, but there's something climbing up your table,' and with one loud *Worraworraworraworraworra* he jumped at the end of the tablecloth, pulled it to the ground, wrapped himself up in it three times, rolled to the other end of the room, and, after a terrible struggle, got his head into the daylight again, and said cheerfully: 'Have I won?'

'That's my tablecloth,' said Pooh, as he began to unwind Tigger.

'I wondered what it was,' said Tigger.

'It goes on the table and you put things on it.'

'Then why did it try to bite me when I wasn't looking?'

'I don't *think* it did,' said Pooh.

'It tried,' said Tigger, 'but I was too quick for it.'

Pooh put the cloth back on the table, and he put a large honey-pot on the cloth, and they sat down to breakfast. And as soon as they sat down, Tigger took a large mouthful of honey . . . and he looked up at the ceiling with his head on one side, and made exploring noises with his tongue, and considering noises, and what-have-we-got-*here* noises . . . and then he said in a very decided voice:

'Tiggers don't like honey.'

'Oh!' said Pooh, and tried to make it sound Sad and Regretful. 'I thought they liked everything.'

'Everything except honey,' said Tigger.

Pooh felt rather pleased about this, and said that, as soon as he had finished his own breakfast, he would take Tigger round to Piglet's house, and Tigger could try some of Piglet's haycorns.

'Thank you, Pooh,' said Tigger, 'because haycorns is really what Tiggers like best.'

So after breakfast they went round to see Piglet, and Pooh explained as they went that Piglet was a Very Small Animal who didn't like bouncing, and asked Tigger not to be too Bouncy just at first. And Tigger, who had been hiding behind trees and jumping out on Pooh's shadow when it wasn't looking, said that Tiggers were only bouncy before breakfast, and that as soon as they had had a few haycorns they became Quiet and Refined. So by-and-by they knocked at the door of Piglet's house.

'Hallo, Pooh,' said Piglet.

'Hallo, Piglet. This is Tigger.'

'Oh, is it?' said Piglet, and he edged round to the other side of the table. 'I thought Tiggers were smaller than that.'

'Not the big ones,' said Tigger.

'They like haycorns,' said Pooh, 'so that's what we've
come for, because poor Tigger hasn't had any breakfast yet.'

Piglet pushed the bowl of haycorns towards Tigger, and said, 'Help yourself,' and then he got close up to Pooh and felt much braver, and said, 'So you're Tigger? Well, well!' in a careless sort of voice. But Tigger said nothing because his mouth was full of haycorns . . .

After a long munching noise he said:

'Ee-ers o i a-ors.'

And when Pooh and Piglet said 'What?' he said 'Skoos ee,' and went outside for a moment.

When he came back he said firmly:

'Tiggers don't like haycorns.'

'But you said they liked everything except honey,' said Pooh.

'Everything except honey and haycorns,' explained Tigger.

When he heard this, Pooh said, 'Oh, I see!' and Piglet, who was rather glad that Tiggers didn't like haycorns, said, 'What about thistles?'

'Thistles,' said Tigger, 'is what Tiggers like best.'

'Then let's go along and see Eeyore,' said Piglet.

So the three of them went; and after they had walked and walked and walked, they came to the part of the Forest where Eeyore was.

'Hallo, Eeyore!' said Pooh. 'This is Tigger.'

'What is?' said Eeyore.

'This,' explained Pooh and Piglet together, and Tigger smiled his happiest smile and said nothing.

Eeyore walked all round Tigger one way, and then turned and walked all round him the other way.

'What did you say it was?' he asked.

'Tigger.'

'Ah!' said Eeyore.

'He's just come,' explained Piglet.

'Ah!' said Eeyore again.

He thought for a long time and then said:

'When is he going?'

Pooh explained to Eeyore that Tigger was a great friend of Christopher Robin's, who had come to stay in the Forest, and Piglet explained to Tigger that he mustn't mind what Eeyore said because he was *always* gloomy; and Eeyore explained to Piglet that, on the contrary, he was feeling particularly cheerful this morning; and Tigger explained to anybody who was listening that he hadn't had any breakfast yet.

'I knew there was something,' said Pooh. 'Tiggers always eat thistles, so that was why we came to see you, Eeyore.'

'Don't mention it, Pooh.'

'Oh, Eeyore, I didn't mean that I didn't *want* to see you –'

'Quite – quite. But your new stripy friend – naturally, he wants his breakfast. What did you say his name was?'

'Tigger.'

'Then come this way, Tigger.'

Eeyore led the way to the most thistly-looking patch of thistles that ever was, and waved a hoof at it.

'A little patch I was keeping for my birthday,' he said, 'but, after all, what *are* birthdays? Here to-day and gone to-morrow. Help yourself, Tigger.'

Tigger thanked him and looked a little anxiously at Pooh.

'Are these really thistles?' he whispered.

'Yes,' said Pooh.

'What Tiggers like best?'

'That's right,' said Pooh.

'I see,' said Tigger.

'So he took a large mouthful, and he gave a large crunch.

'*Ow!*' said Tigger.

He sat down and put his paw in his mouth.

'What's the matter?' asked Pooh.

'*Hot!*' mumbled Tigger.

'Your friend,' said Eeyore, 'appears to have bitten on a bee.'

Pooh's friend stopped shaking his head to get the prickles out, and explained that Tiggers didn't like thistles.

'Then why bend a perfectly good one?' asked Eeyore.

'But you said,' began Pooh, '– you *said* that Tiggers liked everything except honey and haycorns.'

'*And* thistles,' said Tigger, who was now running round in circles with his tongue hanging out.

Pooh looked at him sadly.

'What are we going to do?' he asked Piglet.

Piglet knew the answer to that, and he said at once that they must go and see Christopher Robin.

'You'll find him with Kanga,' said Eeyore. He came close to Pooh, and said in a loud whisper:

'*Could* you ask your friend to do his exercises somewhere else? I shall be having lunch directly, and don't want it bounced on just before I begin. A trifling matter, and fussy of me, but we all have our little ways.'

Pooh nodded solemnly and called to Tigger.

'Come along and we'll go and see Kanga. She's sure to have lots of breakfast for you.'

Tigger finished his last circle and came up to Pooh and Piglet.

'Hot!' he explained with a large and friendly smile. 'Come on!' and he rushed off.

Pooh and Piglet walked slowly after him. And as they walked Piglet said nothing, because he couldn't think of anything, and Pooh said nothing, because he was thinking of a poem. And when he had thought of it he began:

What shall we do about poor little Tigger?
If he never eats nothing he'll never get bigger.
He doesn't like honey and haycorns and thistles
Because of the taste and because of the bristles.
And all the good things which an animal likes
Have the wrong sort of swallow or too many spikes.

'He's quite big enough anyhow,' said Piglet.

'He isn't *really* very big.'

'Well, he *seems* so.'

Pooh was thoughtful when he heard this, and then he murmured to himself:

> But whatever his weight in pounds, shillings, and ounces,
> He always seems bigger because of his bounces.

'And that's the whole poem,' he said. 'Do you like it, Piglet?'

'All except the shillings,' said Piglet. 'I don't think they ought to be there.'

'They wanted to come in after the pounds,' explained Pooh, 'so I let them. It is the best way to write poetry, letting things come.'

'Oh, I didn't know,' said Piglet.

Tigger had been bouncing in front of them all this time, turning round every now and then to ask, 'Is this the way?' – and now at last they came in sight of Kanga's house, and there was Christopher Robin. Tigger rushed up to him.

'Oh, there you are, Tigger!' said Christopher Robin. 'I knew you'd be somewhere.'

'I've been finding things in the Forest,' said Tigger importantly. 'I've found a pooh and a piglet and an eeyore, but I can't find any breakfast.'

Pooh and Piglet came up and hugged Christopher Robin, and explained what had been happening.

'Don't *you* know what Tiggers like?' asked Pooh.

'I expect if I thought very hard I should,' said Christopher Robin, 'but I *thought* Tigger knew.'

'I do,' said Tigger. 'Everything there is in the world except honey and haycorns and – what were those hot things called?'

'Thistles.'

'Yes, and those.'

'Oh, well then, Kanga can give you some breakfast.'

So they went into Kanga's house, and when Roo had said, 'Hallo, Pooh,' and 'Hallo, Piglet' once, and 'Hallo, Tigger' twice, because he had never said it before and it sounded funny, they told Kanga what they wanted, and Kanga said very kindly, 'Well, look in my cupboard, Tigger dear, and see what you'd like.' Because she knew at once that, however big Tigger seemed to be, he wanted as much kindness as Roo.

'Shall I look, too?' said Pooh, who was beginning to feel a little eleven o'clockish. And he found a small tin of condensed milk, and something seemed to tell him that

Tiggers didn't like this, so he took it into a corner by itself, and went with it to see that nobody interrupted it.

But the more Tigger put his nose into this and his paw into that, the more things he found which Tiggers didn't like. And when he had found everything in the cupboard, and couldn't eat any of it, he said to Kanga, 'What happens now?'

But Kanga and Christopher Robin and Piglet were all standing round Roo, watching him have his Extract of Malt. And Roo was saying, 'Must I?' and Kanga was saying, 'Now, Roo dear, you remember what you promised.'

'What is it?' whispered Tigger to Piglet.

'His Strengthening Medicine,' said Piglet. 'He hates it.'

So Tigger came closer, and he leant over the back of Roo's chair, and suddenly he put out his tongue, and took one large golollop, and, with a sudden jump of surprise, Kanga said, 'Oh!' and then clutched at the spoon again just as it was disappearing, and pulled it safely back out of Tigger's mouth. But the Extract of Malt had gone.

'Tigger *dear!*' said Kanga.

'He's taken my medicine, he's taken my medicine, he's taken my medicine!' sang Roo happily, thinking it was a tremendous joke.

Then Tigger looked up at the ceiling, and closed his eyes, and his tongue went round and round his chops, in case he had left any outside, and a peaceful smile came over his face as he said, 'So *that's* what Tiggers like!'

* * *

Which explains why he always lived at Kanga's house afterwards, and had Extract of Malt for breakfast, dinner, and tea. And sometimes, when Kanga thought he wanted strengthening, he had a spoonful or two of Roo's breakfast after meals as medicine.

'But *I* think,' said Piglet to Pooh, 'that he's been strengthened quite enough.'

CHAPTER THREE

*in which a search is organdized,
and Piglet nearly meets
the Heffalump again*

POOH WAS SITTING in his house one day, counting his pots of honey, when there came a knock on the door.

'Fourteen,' said Pooh. 'Come in. Fourteen. Or was it fifteen? Bother. That's muddled me.'

'Hallo, Pooh,' said Rabbit.

'Hallo, Rabbit. Fourteen, wasn't it?'

'What was?'

'My pots of honey what I was counting.'

'Fourteen, that's right.'

'Are you sure?'

'No,' said Rabbit. 'Does it matter?'

'I just like to know,' said Pooh humbly. 'So as I can say to myself: "I've got fourteen pots of honey left." Or fifteen, as the case may be. It's sort of comforting.'

'Well, let's call it sixteen,' said Rabbit. 'What I came to say was: Have you seen Small anywhere about?'

'I don't think so,' said Pooh. And then, after thinking a little more, he said: 'Who is Small?'

'One of my friends-and-relations,' said Rabbit carelessly.

This didn't help Pooh much, because Rabbit had so many friends-and-relations, and of such different sorts and sizes, that he didn't know whether he ought to be looking for Small at the top of an oak-tree or in the petal of a buttercup.

'I haven't seen anybody to-day,' said Pooh, 'not so as to say "Hallo, Small!" to. Did you want him for anything?'

'I don't *want* him,' said Rabbit. 'But it's always useful to know where a friend-and-relation *is*, whether you want him or whether you don't.'

'Oh, I see,' said Pooh. 'Is he lost?'

'Well,' said Rabbit, 'nobody has seen him for a long time, so I suppose he is. Anyhow,' he went on importantly, 'I promised Christopher Robin I'd Organize a Search for him, so come on.'

Pooh said good-bye affectionately to his fourteen pots of honey, and hoped they were fifteen; and he and Rabbit went out into the Forest.

'Now,' said Rabbit, 'this is a Search, and I've Organized it –'

'Done what to it?' said Pooh.

'Organized it. Which means – well, it's what you do to a Search, when you don't all look in the same place at once. So I want *you*, Pooh, to search by the Six Pine Trees first, and then work your way towards Owl's House, and look out for me there. Do you see?'

'No,' said Pooh. 'What –'

'Then I'll see you at Owl's House in about an hour's time.'

'Is Piglet organdized too?'

'We all are,' said Rabbit, and off he went.

* * *

As soon as Rabbit was out of sight, Pooh remembered that he had forgotten to ask who Small was, and

whether he was the sort of friend-and-relation who settled on one's nose, or the sort who got trodden on by mistake, and as it was Too Late Now, he thought he would begin the Hunt by looking for Piglet, and asking him what they were looking for before he looked for it.

'And it's no good looking at the Six Pine Trees for Piglet,' said Pooh to himself, 'because he's been organdized in a special place of his own. So I shall have to look for the Special Place first. I wonder where it is.' And he wrote it down in his head like this:

ORDER OF LOOKING FOR THINGS.

1. Special Place.	(To find Piglet.)
2. Piglet.	(To find who Small is.)
3. Small.	(To find Small.)
4. Rabbit.	(To tell him I've found Small.)
5. Small Again.	(To tell him I've found Rabbit.)

'Which makes it look like a bothering sort of day,' thought Pooh, as he stumped along.

The next moment the day became very bothering indeed, because Pooh was so busy not looking where he was going that he stepped on a piece of the Forest which had been left out by mistake; and he only just had time to think to himself: 'I'm flying. What Owl does.

I wonder how you stop –'
when he stopped.

Bump!

'Ow!' squeaked something.

'That's funny,' thought
Pooh. 'I said "Ow!" without
really oo'ing.'

'Help!' said a small, high voice.

'That's me again,' thought
Pooh. 'I've had an Accident, and
fallen down a well, and my voice has gone all
squeaky and works before I'm ready for it, because I've
done something to myself inside. Bother!'

'Help – help!'

'There you are! I say things when I'm not trying. So
it must be a very bad Accident.' And then he thought
that perhaps when he did try to say things he wouldn't
be able to; so, to make sure, he said loudly: 'A Very Bad
Accident to Pooh Bear.'

'Pooh!' squeaked the voice.

'It's Piglet!' cried Pooh eagerly.
'Where are you?'

'Underneath,' said Piglet in an
underneath sort of way.

'Underneath what?'

'You,' squeaked Piglet. 'Get up!'

'Oh!' said Pooh, and scrambled up as quickly as he could. 'Did I fall on you, Piglet?'

'You fell on me,' said Piglet, feeling himself all over.

'I didn't mean to,' said Pooh sorrowfully.

'I didn't mean to be underneath,' said Piglet sadly. 'But I'm all right now, Pooh, and I *am* so glad it was you.'

'What's happened?' said Pooh. 'Where are we?'

'I think we're in a sort of Pit. I was walking along, looking for somebody, and then suddenly I wasn't any more, and just when I got up to see where I was, something fell on me. And it was you.'

'So it was', said Pooh.

'Yes,' said Piglet. 'Pooh,' he went on nervously, and came a little closer, 'do you think we're in a Trap?'

Pooh hadn't thought about it at all, but now he nodded. For suddenly he remembered how he and Piglet had once made a Pooh Trap for Heffalumps, and he guessed what had happened. He and Piglet had fallen into a Heffalump Trap for Poohs! That was what it was.

'What happens when the Heffalump comes?' asked Piglet tremblingly, when he had heard the news.

'Perhaps he won't notice *you*, Piglet,' said Pooh encouragingly, 'because you're a Very Small Animal.'

'But he'll notice *you*, Pooh.'

'He'll notice me, and I shall notice *him*,' said Pooh, thinking it out. 'We'll notice each other for a long time, and then he'll say: "Ho-*ho!*"'

Piglet shivered a little at the thought of that 'Ho-*ho!*' and his ears began to twitch.

'W-what will *you* say?' he asked.

Pooh tried to think of something he would say, but the more he thought, the more he felt that there is no real answer to 'Ho-*ho!*' said by a Heffalump in the sort of voice this Heffalump was going to say it in.

'I shan't say anything,' said Pooh at last. 'I shall just hum to myself, as if I was waiting for something.'

'Then perhaps he'll say "Ho-*ho!*" again?' suggested Piglet anxiously.

'He will,' said Pooh.

Piglet's ears twitched so quickly that he had to lean them against the side of the Trap to keep them quiet.

'He will say it again,' said Pooh, 'and I shall go on humming. And that will Upset him. Because when you say "Ho-*ho!*" twice, in a gloating sort of way, and the other person only hums, you suddenly find, just as you begin to say it the third time that – that – well, you find –'

'What?'

'That it isn't,' said Pooh.

'Isn't what?'

Pooh knew what he meant, but, being a Bear of Very Little Brain, couldn't think of the words.

'Well, it just isn't,' he said again.

'You mean it isn't ho-*ho*-ish any more?' said Piglet hopefully.

Pooh looked at him admiringly and said that that was what he meant – if you went on humming all the time, because you couldn't go on saying 'Ho-*ho*!' for *ever*.

'But he'll say something else,' said Piglet.

'That's just it. He'll say: "What's all this?" And then *I* shall say – and this is a very good idea, Piglet, which I've just thought of – *I* shall say: "It's a trap for a Heffalump which I've made, and I'm waiting for the Heffalump to fall in." And I shall go on humming. That will Unsettle him.'

'Pooh!' cried Piglet, and now it was *his* turn to be the admiring one. 'You've saved us!'

'Have I?' said Pooh, not feeling quite sure.

But Piglet was quite sure; and his mind ran on, and he saw Pooh and the Heffalump talking to each other, and he thought suddenly, and a little sadly, that it *would* have been rather nice if it had been Piglet and the Heffalump talking so grandly to each other, and not

Pooh, much as he loved Pooh; because he really had more brain than Pooh, and the conversation would go better if he and not Pooh were doing one side of it, and it would be comforting afterwards in the evenings to look back on the day when he answered a Heffalump back as bravely as if the Heffalump wasn't there. It seemed so easy now. He knew just what he would say:

HEFFALUMP (*gloatingly*): 'Ho-*ho*!'

PIGLET (*carelessly*): 'Tra-la-la, tra-la-la.'

HEFFALUMP (*surprised, and not quite so sure of himself*): 'Ho-*ho*!'

PIGLET (*more carelessly still*): 'Tiddle-um-tum, tiddle-um-tum.'

HEFFALUMP (*beginning to say Ho-ho and turning it awkwardly into a cough*): 'H'r'm! What's all this?'

PIGLET (*surprised*): 'Hallo! This is a trap I've made, and I'm waiting for a Heffalump to fall into it.'

HEFFALUMP (*greatly disappointed*): 'Oh!' (*After a long silence*): 'Are you sure?'

PIGLET: 'Yes.'

HEFFALUMP: 'Oh!' (*nervously*): 'I – I thought it was a trap *I'd* made to catch Piglets.'

PIGLET (*surprised*): 'Oh, no!'

HEFFALUMP: 'Oh!' (*apologetically*): 'I – I must have got it wrong then.'

PIGLET: 'I'm afraid so.' (*politely*): 'I'm sorry.' (*He goes on humming.*)

HEFFALUMP: 'Well – well – I – well. I suppose I'd better be getting back?'

PIGLET (*looking up carelessly*): 'Must you? Well, if you see Christopher Robin anywhere, you might tell him I want him.'

HEFFALUMP (*eager to please*): 'Certainly! Certainly!' (*He hurries off.*)

POOH (*who wasn't going to be there, but we find we can't do without him*): 'Oh, Piglet, how brave and clever you are!'

PIGLET (*modestly*): 'Not at all, Pooh.' (*And then, when Christopher Robin comes, Pooh can tell him all about it.*)

While Piglet was dreaming his happy dream, and Pooh was wondering again whether it was fourteen or fifteen, the Search for Small was still going on all over the Forest. Small's real name was Very Small Beetle, but he was called Small for short, when he was spoken to at all, which hardly ever happened except when somebody said: '*Really*, Small!' He had been staying with Christopher Robin for a few seconds, and he had started round a

gorse-bush for exercise, but instead of coming back the other way, as expected, he hadn't, so nobody knew where he was.

'I expect he's just gone home,' said Christopher Robin to Rabbit.

'Did he say Good-bye-and-thank-you-for-a-nice-time?' said Rabbit.

'He'd only just said how-do-you-do,' said Christopher Robin.

'Ha!' said Rabbit. After thinking a little, he went on: 'Has he written a letter saying how much he enjoyed himself, and how sorry he was he had to go so suddenly?'

Christopher Robin didn't think he had.

'Ha!' said Rabbit again, and looked very important. 'This is Serious. He is Lost. We must begin the Search at once.'

Christopher Robin, who was thinking of something else, said: 'Where's Pooh?' – but Rabbit had gone. So he went into his house and drew a picture of Pooh going on a long walk at about seven o'clock in the morning, and then he climbed to the top of his tree and climbed down again, and then he wondered what Pooh was doing, and went across the Forest to see.

It was not long before he came to the Gravel Pit, and he looked down, and there were Pooh and Piglet, with their backs to him, dreaming happily.

'Ho-*ho*!' said Christopher Robin loudly and suddenly.

Piglet jumped six inches in the air with Surprise and Anxiety, but Pooh went on dreaming.

'It's the Heffalump!' thought Piglet nervously. 'Now, then!' He hummed in his throat a little, so that none of the words should stick, and then, in the most delightfully easy way, he said: 'Tra-la-la, tra-la-la,' as if he had just thought of it. But he didn't look round, because if you look round and see a Very Fierce Heffalump

looking down at you, sometimes you forget what you were going to say.

'Rum-tum-tum-tiddle-um,' said Christopher Robin in a voice like Pooh's. Because Pooh had once invented a song which went:

Tra-la-la, tra-la-la,
Tra-la-la, tra-la-la,
Rum-tum-tum-tiddle-um.

So whenever Christopher Robin sings it, he always sings it in a Pooh-voice, which seems to suit it better.

'He's said the wrong thing,' thought Piglet anxiously. He ought to have said, 'Ho-*ho*!' again. Perhaps I had better say it for him. And, as fiercely as he could, Piglet said: 'Ho-*ho*!'

'How *did* you get there, Piglet?' said Christopher Robin in his ordinary voice.

'This is Terrible,' thought Piglet. 'First he talks in Pooh's voice, and then he talks in Christopher Robin's voice, and he's doing it so as to Unsettle me. And being now Completely Unsettled, he said very quickly and squeakily: 'This is a trap for Poohs, and I'm waiting to fall in it, ho-*ho*, what's all this, and then I say ho-*ho* again.'

'*What*?' said Christopher Robin.

'A trap for ho-ho's,' said Piglet huskily. 'I've just made it, and I'm waiting for the ho-ho to come-come.'

How long Piglet would have gone on like this I don't know, but at that moment Pooh woke up suddenly and decided that it was sixteen. So he got up; and as he turned his head so as to soothe himself in that awkward place in the middle of the back where something was tickling him, he saw Christopher Robin.

'Hallo!' he shouted joyfully.

'Hallo, Pooh.'

Piglet looked up, and looked away again. And he felt so Foolish and Uncomfortable that he had almost decided to run away to Sea and be a Sailor, when suddenly he saw something.

'Pooh!' he cried. 'There's something climbing up your back.'

'I thought there was,' said Pooh.

'It's Small!' cried Piglet.

'Oh, *that's* who it is, is it?' said Pooh.

'Christopher Robin, I've found Small!' cried Piglet.

'Well done, Piglet,' said Christopher Robin.

And at these encouraging words Piglet felt quite happy again, and decided not to be a Sailor after all. So when Christopher Robin had helped them out of the Gravel Pit, they all went off together hand-in-hand.

And two days later Rabbit happened to meet Eeyore in the Forest.

'Hallo, Eeyore,' he said, 'what are *you* looking for?'

'Small, of course,' said Eeyore. 'Haven't you any brain?'

'Oh, but didn't I tell you?' said Rabbit. 'Small was found two days ago.'

There was a moment's silence.

'Ha-ha,' said Eeyore bitterly. 'Merriment and what-not. Don't apologize. It's just what *would* happen.'

CHAPTER FOUR

in which it is shown
that Tiggers don't climb trees

O NE DAY WHEN POOH was thinking, he thought he would go and see Eeyore, because he hadn't seen him since yesterday. And as he walked through the heather, singing to himself, he suddenly remembered that he hadn't seen Owl since the day before yesterday, so he thought that he would just look in at the Hundred Acre Wood on the way and see if Owl was at home.

Well, he went on singing, until he came to the part of the stream where the stepping-stones were, and when he was in the middle of the third stone he began to wonder how Kanga and Roo and Tigger were getting on, because they all lived together in a different part of the Forest. And he thought, 'I haven't seen Roo for a long time, and if I don't see him today it will be a still longer time.' So he sat down on the stone in the middle of the stream, and sang another verse of his song, while he wondered what to do.

The other verse of the song was like this:

> I could spend a happy morning
> Seeing Roo,
> I could spend a happy morning
> Being Pooh.
> For it doesn't seem to matter,
> If I don't get any fatter
> (And I *don't* get any fatter),
> What I do.

The sun was so delightfully warm, and the stone, which had been sitting in it for a long time, was so warm, too, that Pooh had almost decided to go on being Pooh in the middle of the stream for the rest of the morning, when he remembered Rabbit.

'Rabbit,' said Pooh to himself. 'I *like* talking to Rabbit. He talks about sensible things. He doesn't use long, difficult words, like Owl. He uses short, easy words, like "What about lunch?" and "Help yourself, Pooh." I suppose, *really*, I ought to go and see Rabbit.'

Which made him think of another verse:

> Oh, I like his way of talking,
>   Yes, I do.
> It's the nicest way of talking
>   Just for two.
> And a Help-yourself with Rabbit
> Though it may become a habit,
> Is a pleasant sort of habit
>   For a Pooh.

So when he had sung this, he got up off his stone, walked back across the stream, and set off for Rabbit's house.

But he hadn't got far before he began to say to himself:

'Yes, but suppose Rabbit is out?'

'Or suppose I get stuck in his front door again, coming out, as I did once when his front door wasn't big enough?'

'Because I *know* I'm not getting fatter, but his front door may be getting thinner.'

'So wouldn't it be better if –'

And all the time he was saying things like this he was going more and more westerly, without thinking . . . until suddenly he found himself at his own front door again.

And it was eleven o'clock.

Which was Time-for-a-little-something . . .

Half an hour later he was doing what he had always really meant to do, he was stumping off to Piglet's house. And as he walked, he wiped his mouth with the back of his paw, and sang rather a fluffy song through the fur. It went like this:

> I could spend a happy morning
>> Seeing Piglet.
> And I couldn't spend a happy morning
>> Not seeing Piglet.
> And it doesn't seem to matter
> If I don't see Owl and Eeyore
>> (or any of the others),

And I'm not going to see Owl or Eeyore
(or any of the others)
Or Christopher Robin.

Written down like this, it doesn't seem a very good song, but coming through pale fawn fluff at about half-past eleven on a very sunny morning, it seemed to Pooh to be one of the best songs he had ever sung. So he went on singing it.

Piglet was busy digging a small hole in the ground outside his house.

'Hallo, Piglet,' said Pooh.

'Hallo, Pooh,' said Piglet, giving a jump of surprise. 'I knew it was you.'

'So did I,' said Pooh. 'What are you doing?'

'I'm planting a haycorn, Pooh, so that it can grow up into an oak-tree, and have lots of haycorns just outside the front door instead of having to walk miles and miles, do you see, Pooh?'

'Supposing it doesn't?' said Pooh.

'It will, because Christopher Robin says it will, so that's why I'm planting it.'

'Well,' said Pooh, 'if I plant a honeycomb outside my house, then it will grow up into a beehive.'

Piglet wasn't quite sure about this.

'Or a *piece* of a honeycomb,' said Pooh, 'so as not to waste too much. Only then I might only get a piece of a beehive, and it might be the wrong piece, where the bees were buzzing and not hunnying. Bother.'

Piglet agreed that that would be rather bothering.

'Besides, Pooh, it's a very difficult thing, planting unless you know how to do it,' he said; and he put the acorn in the hole he had made,

and covered it up with earth,

and jumped on it.

'I do know,' said Pooh, 'because Christopher Robin gave me a mastershalum seed, and I planted it, and I'm going to have mastershalums all over the front door.'

'I thought they were called nasturtiums,' said Piglet timidly, as he went on jumping.

'No,' said Pooh. 'Not these. These are called mastershalums.'

When Piglet had finished jumping, he wiped his paws on his front, and said, 'What shall we do now?' and Pooh said, 'Let's go and see Kanga and Roo and Tigger,' and Piglet said, 'Y-yes. L-lets' – because he was still a little anxious about Tigger, who was a very Bouncy Animal, with a way of saying How-do-you-do, which always left your ears full of sand, even after Kanga had said, 'Gently, Tigger dear,' and had helped you up again. So they set off for Kanga's house.

* * *

Now it happened that Kanga had felt rather motherly that morning, and Wanting to Count Things – like Roo's vests, and how many pieces of soap there were left, and the two clean spots in Tigger's feeder; so she had sent them out with a packet of watercress sandwiches for Roo and a packet of extract-of-malt sandwiches for Tigger, to have a nice long morning in the Forest not getting into mischief. And off they had gone.

And as they went, Tigger told Roo (who wanted to know) all about the things that Tiggers could do.

'Can they fly?' asked Roo.

'Yes,' said Tigger, 'they're very good flyers, Tiggers are. Strornry good flyers.'

'Oo!' said Roo. 'Can they fly as well as Owl?'

'Yes,' said Tigger. 'Only they don't want to.'

'Why don't they want to?'

'Well, they just don't like it, somehow.'

Roo couldn't understand this, because he thought it would be lovely to be able to fly, but Tigger said it was difficult to explain to anybody who wasn't a Tigger himself.

'Well,' said Roo, 'can they jump as far as Kangas?'

'Yes,' said Tigger. 'When they want to.'

'I *love* jumping,' said Roo. 'Let's see who can jump farthest, you or me.'

'I can,' said Tigger. 'But we mustn't stop now, or we shall be late.'

'Late for what?'

'For whatever we want to be in time for,' said Tigger, hurrying on.

In a little while they came to the Six Pine Trees.

'I can swim,' said Roo. 'I fell into the river, and I swimmed. Can Tiggers swim?'

'Of course they can. Tiggers can do everything.'

'Can they climb trees better than Pooh?' asked Roo, stopping under the tallest Pine Tree, and looking up at it.

'Climbing trees is what they do best,' said Tigger. 'Much better than Poohs.'

'Could they climb this one?'

'They're always climbing trees like that,' said Tigger. 'Up and down all day.'

'Oo, Tigger, are they *really*?'

'I'll show you,' said Tigger bravely, 'and you can sit on my back and watch me.' For of all the things which he had said Tiggers could do, the only one he felt really certain about suddenly was climbing trees.

'Oo, Tigger – oo, Tigger – oo, Tigger!' squeaked Roo excitedly.

So he sat on Tigger's back and up they went.

And for the first ten feet Tigger said happily to himself, 'Up we go!'

And for the next ten feet he said:

'I always *said* Tiggers could climb trees.'

And for the next ten feet he said:

'Not that it's easy, mind you.'

And for the next ten feet he said:

'Of course, there's the coming-down too. Backwards.'

And then he said:

'Which will be difficult . . . '

'Unless one fell . . . '

'When it would be . . . '

'EASY.'

And at the word 'easy', the branch he was standing on broke suddenly and he just managed to clutch at the one above him as he felt himself going . . . and then slowly he got his chin over it . . . and then one back paw . . . and then the other . . . until at last he was sitting on it, breathing very quickly, and wishing that he had gone in for swimming instead.

Roo climbed off, and sat down next to him.

'Oo, Tigger,' he said excitedly, 'are we at the top?'

'No,' said Tigger.

'Are we going to the top?'

'No,' said Tigger.

'Oh!' said Roo rather sadly. And then he went on hopefully: 'That was a lovely bit just now, when you pretended we were going to fall-bump-to-the-bottom, and we didn't. Will you do that bit again?'

'NO,' said Tigger.

Roo was silent for a little while, and then he said, 'Shall we eat our sandwiches, Tigger?' And Tigger said, 'Yes, where are they?' And Roo said, 'At the bottom of the tree.' And Tigger said, 'I don't think we'd better eat them just yet.' So they didn't.

By-and-by Pooh and Piglet came along. Pooh was telling Piglet in a singing voice that it didn't seem to matter, if he didn't get any fatter, and he didn't *think* he was getting any fatter, what he did; and Piglet was wondering how long it would be before his haycorn came up.

'Look, Pooh!' said Piglet suddenly. 'There's something in one of the Pine Trees.'

'So there is!' said Pooh, looking up wonderingly. 'There's an Animal.'

Piglet took Pooh's arm, in case Pooh was frightened.

'Is it One of the Fiercer Animals?' he said, looking the other way.

Pooh nodded.

'It's a Jagular,' he said.

'What do Jagulars do?' asked Piglet, hoping that they wouldn't.

'They hide in the branches of trees, and drop on you as you go underneath,' said Pooh. 'Christopher Robin told me.'

'Perhaps we better hadn't go underneath, Pooh. In case he dropped and hurt himself.'

'They don't hurt themselves,' said Pooh. 'They're such very good droppers.'

Piglet still felt that to be underneath a Very Good Dropper would be a Mistake, and he was just going to hurry back for something which he had forgotten when the Jagular called out to them.

'Help! Help!' it called.

'That's what Jagulars always do,' said Pooh, much interested. 'They call "Help! Help!" and then when you look up, they drop on you.'

'I'm looking *down*,' cried Piglet loudly, so as the Jagular shouldn't do the wrong thing by accident.

Something very excited next to the Jagular heard him and squeaked:

'Pooh and Piglet! Pooh and Piglet!'

All of a sudden Piglet felt that it was a much nicer day than he had thought it was. All warm and sunny –

'Pooh!' he cried. 'I believe it's Tigger and Roo!'

'So it is,' said Pooh. 'I thought it was a Jagular and another Jagular.'

'Hallo, Roo!' called Piglet. 'What are you doing?'

'We can't get down, we can't get down!' cried Roo. 'Isn't it fun? Pooh, isn't it fun, Tigger and I are living in a tree, like Owl, and we're going to stay here for ever and ever. I can see Piglet's house. Piglet, I can see your house from here. Aren't we high? Is Owl's house as high up as this?'

'How did you get there, Roo?' asked Piglet.

'On Tigger's back! And Tiggers can't climb downwards, because their tails get in the way, only upwards, and Tigger forgot about that when we started, and he's only just remembered. So we've got to stay here forever and ever – unless we go higher. What did you say, Tigger? Oh, Tigger says if we go higher we shan't be able to see Piglet's house so well, so we're going to stop here.'

'Piglet,' said Pooh solemnly, when he had heard all this, 'what shall we do?' And he began to eat Tigger's sandwiches.

'Are they stuck?' asked Piglet anxiously.

Pooh nodded.

'Couldn't you climb up to them?'

'I might, Piglet, and I might bring Roo down on my back, but I couldn't bring Tigger down. So we must think of something else.' And in a thoughtful way he began to eat Roo's sandwiches, too.

* * *

Whether he would have thought of anything before he had finished the last sandwich, I don't know, but he had just got to the last but one when there was a crackling in the bracken, and Christopher Robin and Eeyore came strolling along together.

'I shouldn't be surprised if it hailed a good deal to-morrow,' Eeyore was saying. 'Blizzards and what-not. Being fine today doesn't Mean Anything. It has no sig – what's that word? Well, it has none of that. It's just a small piece of weather.'

'There's Pooh!' said Christopher Robin, who didn't much mind *what* it did tomorrow, as long as he was out in it. 'Hallo, Pooh!'

'It's Christopher Robin!' said Piglet. '*He'll* know what to do.'

They hurried up to him.

'Oh, Christopher Robin,' began Pooh.

'And Eeyore,' said Eeyore.

'Tigger and Roo are right up the Six Pine Trees, and they can't get down, and –'

'And I was just saying,' put in Piglet, 'that if only Christopher Robin –'

'*And* Eeyore –'

'If only you were here, then we could think of something to do.'

Christopher Robin looked up at Tigger and Roo, and tried to think of something.

'*I* thought,' said Piglet earnestly, 'that if Eeyore stood at the bottom of the tree, and if Pooh stood on Eeyore's back, and if I stood on Pooh's shoulders –'

'And if Eeyore's back snapped suddenly, then we could all laugh. Ha Ha! Amusing in a quiet way,' said Eeyore, 'but not really helpful.'

'Well,' said Piglet meekly, '*I* thought –'

'Would it break your back, Eeyore?' asked Pooh, very much surprised.

'That's what would be so interesting, Pooh. Not being quite sure till afterwards.'

Pooh said 'Oh!' and they all began to think again.

'I've got an idea!' cried Christopher Robin suddenly.

'Listen to this, Piglet,' said Eeyore, 'and then you'll know what we're trying to do.'

'I'll take off my tunic and we'll each hold a corner, and then Roo and Tigger can jump into it, and it will be all soft and bouncy for them, and they won't hurt themselves.'

'*Getting Tigger down*,' said Eeyore, 'and *Not hurting anybody*. Keep those two ideas in your head, Piglet, and you'll be all right.'

But Piglet wasn't listening, he was so agog at

the thought of seeing Christopher Robin's blue braces again. He had only seen them once before, when he was much younger, and, being a little over-excited by them, had had to go to bed half an hour earlier than usual; and he had always wondered since if they were *really* as blue and as bracing as he had thought them. So when Christopher Robin took his tunic off, and they were, he felt quite friendly to Eeyore again, and held the corner of the tunic next to him and smiled happily at him. And Eeyore whispered back: 'I'm not saying there won't be an Accident *now*, mind you. They're funny things, Accidents. You never have them till you're having them.'

When Roo understood what he had to do, he was wildly excited, and cried out: 'Tigger, Tigger, we're going to jump! Look at me jumping, Tigger! Like flying, my jumping will be. Can Tiggers do it?' And he squeaked out: 'I'm coming, Christopher Robin!' and he jumped – straight into the middle of the tunic. And he was going so fast that he bounced up again almost as high as where he was before – and went on bouncing and saying 'Oo!' for quite a long time – and then at last he stopped and said, 'Oo, lovely!' And they put him on the ground.

'Come on, Tigger,' he called out. 'It's easy.'

But Tigger was holding on to the branch and saying to himself: 'It's all very well for Jumping Animals like Kangas, but it's quite different for Swimming Animals like Tiggers.' And he thought of himself floating on his back down a river, or striking out from one island to another, and he felt that that was really the life for a Tigger.'

'Come along,' called Christopher Robin. 'You'll be all right.'

'Just wait a moment,' said Tigger nervously. 'Small piece of bark in my eye.' And he moved slowly along his branch.

'Come on, it's easy!' squeaked Roo. And suddenly Tigger found how easy it was.

'Ow!' he shouted as the tree flew past him.

'Look out!' cried Christopher Robin to the others.

There was a crash, and a tearing noise, and a confused heap of everybody on the ground.

Christopher Robin and Pooh and Piglet picked themselves up first, and then they picked Tigger up, and underneath everybody else was Eeyore.

'Oh, Eeyore!' cried Christopher Robin. 'Are you hurt?' And he felt him rather anxiously, and dusted him and helped him to stand up again.

Eeyore said nothing for a long time. And then he said: 'Is Tigger there?'

Tigger was there, feeling Bouncy again already.

'Yes,' said Christopher Robin. 'Tigger's here.'

'Well, just thank him for me,' said Eeyore.

CHAPTER FIVE

in which Rabbit has a busy day,
and we learn what Christopher Robin
does in the mornings

IT WAS GOING to be one of Rabbit's busy days. As soon as he woke up he felt important, as if everything depended upon him. It was just the day for Organizing Something, or for Writing a Notice Signed Rabbit, or for Seeing What Everybody Else Thought About It. It was a perfect morning for hurrying round to Pooh, and saying, 'Very well, then, I'll tell Piglet,' and then going to Piglet, and saying, 'Pooh thinks – but perhaps I'd better see Owl first.' It was a Captainish sort of day, when everybody said, 'Yes, Rabbit' and 'No, Rabbit,' and waited until he had told them.

He came out of his house and sniffed the warm spring morning as he wondered what he would do. Kanga's house was nearest, and at Kanga's house was Roo, who said 'Yes, Rabbit' and 'No, Rabbit' almost better

than anybody else in the Forest; but there was another animal there nowadays, the strange and Bouncy Tigger; and he was the sort of Tigger who was always in front when you were showing him the way anywhere, and was generally out of sight when at last you came to the place and said proudly, 'Here we are!'

'No, not Kanga's,' said Rabbit thoughtfully to himself, as he curled his whiskers in the sun; and, to make quite sure that he wasn't going there, he turned to the left and trotted off in the other direction, which was the way to Christopher Robin's house.

'After all,' said Rabbit to himself, 'Christopher Robin depends on Me. He's fond of Pooh and Piglet and Eeyore, and so am I, but they haven't any Brain. Not to notice. And he respects Owl, because you can't help respecting anybody who can spell TUESDAY, even if he doesn't spell it right; but spelling isn't everything. There are days when spelling Tuesday simply doesn't count. And Kanga is too busy looking after Roo, and Roo is too young and Tigger is too bouncy to be of any help, so there's really nobody but Me, when you come to look at it. I'll go and see if there's anything he wants doing, and then I'll do it for him. It's just the day for doing things.'

He trotted along happily, and by-the-by he crossed the stream and came to the place where his friends-and-relations lived. There seemed to be even more of them about than usual this morning, and having nodded to a hedgehog or two, with whom he was too busy to shake hands and having said, 'Good morning, good morning,' importantly to some of the others, and 'Ah, there you are,' kindly, to the smaller ones, he waved a paw at them over his shoulder, and was gone; leaving such an air of excitement and I-don't-know-what behind him, that several members of the Beetle family, including Henry Rush, made their way at once to the Hundred Acre Wood and began climbing trees, in the hope of getting to the top before it happened, whatever it was, so that they might see it properly.

Rabbit hurried on by the edge of the Hundred Acre Wood, feeling more important every minute, and soon he came to the tree where Christopher Robin lived. He knocked at the door, and he called out once or twice, and then he walked back a little way and put his paw up to keep the sun out, and called to the top of the tree, and then he turned all round and shouted 'Hallo!' and 'I say!' 'It's Rabbit!' – but nothing happened.

Then he stopped and listened, and everything stopped and listened with him, and the Forest was very lone and still and peaceful in the sunshine, until suddenly a hundred miles above him a lark began to sing.

'Bother!' said Rabbit. 'He's gone out.'

He went back to the green front door, just to make sure, and he was turning away, feeling that his morning had got all spoilt, when he saw a piece of paper on the ground. And there was a pin in it, as if it had fallen off the door.

'Ha!' said Rabbit, feeling quite happy again. 'Another notice!'

This is what it said:

GON OUT
BACKSON
BISY
BACKSON
C.R.

'Ha!' said Rabbit again. 'I must tell the others.' And he hurried off importantly.

The nearest house was Owl's, and to Owl's House in the Hundred Acre Wood he made his way. He came to Owl's door, and he knocked and he rang, and he rang and he knocked, and at last Owl's head came out and said, 'Go away, I'm thinking – oh, it's you?' which was how he always began.

'Owl,' said Rabbit shortly, 'you and I have brains. The others have fluff. If there is any thinking to be done in this Forest – and when I say thinking I mean *thinking* – you and I must do it.'

'Yes,' said Owl. 'I was.'

'Read that.'

Owl took Christopher Robin's notice from Rabbit and looked at it nervously. He could spell his own name WOL, and he could spell Tuesday so that you knew it wasn't Wednesday, and he could read quite comfortably when you weren't looking over his shoulder and saying

'Well?' all the time, and he could –

'Well?' said Rabbit.

'Yes,' said Owl, looking Wise and Thoughtful. 'I see what you mean. Undoubtedly.'

'Well?'

'Exactly,' said Owl. 'Precisely.' And he added, after a little thought, 'If you had not come to me, I should have come to you.'

'Why?' asked Rabbit.

'For that very reason,' said Owl, hoping that something helpful would happen soon.

'Yesterday morning,' said Rabbit solemnly, 'I went to see Christopher Robin. He was out. Pinned on his door was a notice!'

'The same notice?'

'A different one. But the meaning was the same. It's very odd.'

'Amazing,' said Owl, looking at the notice again, and getting, just for a moment, a curious sort of feeling that something had happened to Christopher Robin's back. 'What did you do?'

'Nothing.'

'The best thing,' said Owl wisely.

'Well?' said Rabbit again, as Owl knew he was going to.

'Exactly,' said Owl.

For a little while he couldn't think of anything more; and then, all of a sudden, he had an idea.

'Tell me, Rabbit,' he said, 'the *exact* words of the first notice. This is very important. Everything depends on this. The *exact* words of the *first* notice.'

'It was just the same as that one really.'

Owl looked at him, and wondered whether to push him off the tree; but, feeling that he could always do it afterwards, he tried once more to find out what they were talking about.

'The exact words, please,' he said, as if Rabbit hadn't spoken.

'It just said, "Gon out. Backson." Same as this, only this says "Bisy Backson" too.'

Owl gave a great sigh of relief.

'Ah!' said Owl. '*Now* we know where we are.'

'Yes, but where's Christopher Robin?' said Rabbit. 'That's the point.'

Owl looked at the notice again. To one of his education the reading of it was easy. 'Gon out, Backson. Bisy, Backson' – just the sort of thing you'd expect to see on a notice.

'It is quite clear what has happened, my dear Rabbit,'

he said. 'Christopher Robin has gone out somewhere with Backson. He and Backson are busy together. Have you seen a Backson anywhere about in the Forest lately?'

'I don't know,' said Rabbit. 'That's what I came to ask you. What are they like?'

'Well,' said Owl, 'the Spotted or Herbaceous Backson is just a –'

'At least,' he said, 'it's really more of a –'

'Of course,' he said, 'it depends on the –'

'Well,' said Owl, 'the fact is,' he said, 'I don't know *what* they're like,' said Owl frankly.

'Thank you,' said Rabbit. And he hurried off to see Pooh.

Before he had gone very far he heard a noise. So he stopped and listened. This was the noise:

NOISE, BY POOH

Oh, the butterflies are flying,
Now the winter days are dying,
And the primroses are trying
   To be seen.
And the turtle-doves are cooing,
And the woods are up and doing,
For the violets are blue-ing
   In the green.

Oh, the honey-bees are gumming
On their little wings, and humming
That the summer, which is coming,
    Will be fun.
And the cows are almost cooing,
And the turtle-doves are mooing,
Which is why a Pooh is poohing
    In the sun.

For the spring is really springing;
You can see a skylark singing,
And the blue-bells, which are ringing,
    Can be heard.
And the cuckoo isn't cooing,
But he's cucking and he's ooing,
And a Pooh is simply poohing
    Like a bird.

'Hallo, Pooh,' said Rabbit.

'Hallo, Rabbit,' said Pooh dreamily.

'Did you make that song up?'

'Well, I sort of made it up,' said Pooh. 'It isn't Brain,' he went on humbly, 'because You Know Why, Rabbit; but it comes to me sometimes.'

'Ah!' said Rabbit, who never let things come to him, but always went and fetched them. 'Well, the point is, have you seen a Spotted or Herbaceous Backson in the Forest, at all?'

'No,' said Pooh. 'Not a – no,' said Pooh. 'I saw Tigger just now.'

'That's no good.'

'No,' said Pooh. 'I thought it wasn't.'

'Have you seen Piglet?'

'Yes,' said Pooh. 'I suppose *that* isn't any good either?' he asked meekly.

'Well, it depends if he saw anything.'

'He saw me,' said Pooh.

Rabbit sat down on the ground next to Pooh, and, feeling much less important like that, stood up again.

'What it all comes to is this,' he said, '*What does Christopher Robin do in the morning nowadays?*'

'What sort of thing?'

'Well, can you tell me anything you've seen him do in the morning? These last few days.'

'Yes,' said Pooh. 'We had breakfast together yesterday. By the Pine Trees.

I'd made up a little basket, just a little, fair-sized basket, an ordinary biggish sort of basket, full of –'

'Yes, yes,' said Rabbit, 'but I mean later than that. Have you seen him between eleven and twelve?'

'Well,' said Pooh, 'at eleven o'clock – at eleven o'clock – well, at eleven o'clock, you see, I generally get home about then. Because I have One or Two Things to Do.'

'Quarter past eleven, then?'

'Well –' said Pooh.

'Half past?'

'Yes,' said Pooh. 'At half past – or perhaps later – I might see him.'

And now that he did think of it,

he began to remember that he hadn't seen Christopher Robin about so much lately. Not in the mornings. Afternoons, yes; evenings, yes; before breakfast, yes; just after breakfast, yes. And then, perhaps, 'See you again, Pooh,' and off he'd go.

'That's just it,' said Rabbit. 'Where?'

'Perhaps he's looking for something.'

'What?' asked Rabbit.

'That's just what I was going to say,' said Pooh. And then he added, 'Perhaps he's looking for a – for a –

'A Spotted or Herbaceous Backson?'

'Yes,' said Pooh. 'One of those. In case it isn't.'

Rabbit looked at him severely.

'I don't think you're helping,' he said.

'No,' said Pooh. 'I do try,' he added humbly.

Rabbit thanked him for trying, and said that he would now go and see Eeyore, and Pooh could walk with him if he liked. But Pooh, who felt another verse of his song coming on him, said he would wait for Piglet, good-bye, Rabbit; so Rabbit went off.

But, as it happened, it was Rabbit who saw Piglet first. Piglet had got up early that morning to pick himself a

bunch of violets; and when he had picked them and put them in a pot in the middle of his house, it suddenly came over him that nobody had ever picked Eeyore a bunch of violets, and the more he thought of this, the more he thought how sad it was to be an Animal who had never had a bunch of violets picked for him. So he hurried out again, saying to himself, 'Eeyore, Violets,' and then, 'Violets, Eeyore,' in case he forgot, because it was that sort of day, and he picked a large bunch and trotted along, smelling them, and feeling very happy, until he came to the place where Eeyore was.

'Oh, Eeyore,' began Piglet a little nervously, because Eeyore was busy.

Eeyore put out a paw and waved him away.

'To-morrow,' said Eeyore. 'Or the next day.'

Piglet came a little closer to see what it was. Eeyore had three sticks on the ground, and was looking at them. Two of the sticks were touching at one end, but not at the other, and the third stick was laid across them. Piglet thought that perhaps it was a Trap of some kind.

'Oh, Eeyore,' he began again, 'I just –'

'Is that little Piglet?' said Eeyore, still looking hard at his sticks.

'Yes, Eeyore, and I –'

'Do you know what this is?'

'No,' said Piglet.

'It's an A.'

'Oh,' said Piglet.

'Not O – A,' said Eeyore severely. 'Can't you *hear*, or do you think you have more education than Christopher Robin?'

'Yes,' said Piglet. 'No,' said Piglet very quickly. And he came closer still.

'Christopher Robin said it was an A, and an A it is – until somebody treads on it,' Eeyore added sternly.

Piglet jumped backwards hurriedly, and smelt at his violets.

'Do you know what A means, little Piglet?'

'No, Eeyore, I don't.'

'It means Learning, it means Education, it means all the things that you and Pooh haven't got. That's what A means.'

'Oh,' said Piglet again. 'I mean, does it?' he explained quickly.

'I'm telling you. People come and go in this Forest, and they say, "It's only Eeyore, so it doesn't count." They walk to and fro saying, "Ha-ha!" But do they know anything about A? They don't. It's just three sticks to *them*. But to the Educated – mark this, little Piglet – to the Educated, not meaning Poohs and Piglets, it's a great and glorious A. Not,' he added, 'just something that anybody can come and *breathe* on.'

Piglet stepped back nervously, and looked round for help.

'Here's Rabbit,' he said gladly. 'Hallo, Rabbit.'

Rabbit came up importantly, nodded to Piglet, and said, 'Ah, Eeyore,' in the voice of one who would be saying 'Good-bye' in about two more minutes.

'There's just one thing I wanted to ask you, Eeyore. What happens to Christopher Robin in the mornings nowadays?'

'What's this that I'm looking at?' said Eeyore still looking at it.

'Three sticks,' said Rabbit promptly.

'You see?' said Eeyore to Piglet. He turned to Rabbit. 'I will now answer your question,' he said solemnly.

'Thank you,' said Rabbit.

'What does Christopher Robin do in the mornings? He learns. He becomes Educated. He instigorates – I *think* that is the word he mentioned, but I may be referring to something else – he instigorates Knowledge. In my small way I also, if I have the word right, am – am doing what he does. That, for instance, is –'

'An A,' said Rabbit, 'but not a very good one. Well, I must get back and tell the others.'

Eeyore looked at his sticks and then he looked at Piglet.

'What did Rabbit say it was?' he asked.

'An A,' said Piglet.

'Did you tell him?'

'No, Eeyore, I didn't. I expect he just knew.'

'He *knew*? You mean this A thing is a thing *Rabbit* knew?'

'Yes, Eeyore. He's clever, Rabbit is.'

'Clever!' said Eeyore scornfully, putting a foot heavily on his three sticks. 'Education!' said Eeyore bitterly, jumping on his six sticks. 'What *is* Learning?' asked Eeyore as he kicked his twelve sticks into the air. 'A thing *Rabbit* knows! Ha!'

'I think –' began Piglet nervously.

'Don't,' said Eeyore.

'I think *Violets* are rather nice,' said Piglet. And he laid his bunch in front of Eeyore and scampered off.

* * *

Next morning the notice on Christopher Robin's door said:

GONE OUT
BACK SOON
C.R.

Which is why all the animals in the Forest – except, of course, the Spotted and Herbaceous Backson – now know what Christopher Robin does in the mornings.

CHAPTER SIX

in which Pooh invents a new game
and Eeyore joins in

BY THE TIME IT CAME to the edge of the Forest the stream had grown up, so that it was almost a river, and, being grown-up, it did not run and jump and sparkle along as it used to do when it was younger, but moved more slowly. For it knew now where it was going, and it said to itself, 'There is no hurry. We shall get there some day.' But all the little streams higher up in the Forest went this way and that, quickly, eagerly, having so much to find out before it was too late.

There was a broad track, almost as broad as a road, leading from the Outland to the Forest, but before it could come to the Forest, it had to cross this river. So, where it crossed, there was a wooden bridge, almost as broad as a road, with wooden rails on each side of it. Christopher Robin could just get his chin on to the top rail, if he wanted to, but it was more fun to stand on the bottom rail, so that he could lean right over, and watch the river slipping slowly away beneath him. Pooh could get his chin on to the bottom rail if wanted to, but it was more fun to lie down and get his head under it, and watch the river slipping slowly away beneath him. And this was the only way in which Piglet and Roo could watch the river at all, because they were too small to reach the bottom rail. So they would lie down and watch it . . . and it slipped away very slowly, being in no hurry to get there.

One day, when Pooh was walking towards this bridge, he was trying to make up a piece of poetry about fir-cones, because there they were, lying about on each side of him, and he felt singy. So he picked a fir-cone up,

and looked at it, and said to himself, 'This is a very good fir-cone, and something ought to rhyme to it.' But he couldn't think of anything. And then this came into his head suddenly:

> Here is a myst'ry
> About a little fir-tree.
> Owl says it's *his* tree,
> And Kanga says it's *her* tree.

'Which doesn't make sense,' said Pooh, 'because Kanga doesn't live in a tree.'

He had just come to the bridge; and not looking where he was going, he tripped over something, and the fir-cone jerked out of his paw into the river.

'Bother,' said Pooh, as it floated slowly under the bridge, and he went back to get another fir-cone which had a rhyme to it. But then he thought that he would just look at the river instead, because it was a peaceful sort of day, so he lay down and looked at it, and it slipped slowly away beneath him . . . and suddenly, there was his fir-cone slipping away too.

'That's funny,' said Pooh. 'I dropped it on the other side,' said Pooh, 'and it came out on this side! I wonder if it would do it again?' And he went back for some more fir-cones.

It did. It kept on doing it. Then he dropped two in at once, and leant over the bridge to see which of them would come out first; and one of them did; but as they were both the same size, he didn't know if it was the one which he wanted to win, or the other one. So the next time he dropped one big one and one little one, and the big one came out first, which was what he had said it would do, and the little one came out last, which was what he had said it would do, so he had won twice . . . and when he went home for tea, he had won thirty six and lost twenty-eight, which meant that he was – that he had – well, you take twenty-eight from thirty-six, and *that*'s what he was. Instead of the other way round.

And that was the beginning of the game called Poohsticks, which Pooh invented, and which he and his friends used to play on the edge of the Forest. But they played with sticks instead of fir-cones, because they were easier to mark.

Now one day Pooh and Piglet and Rabbit and Roo were all playing Poohsticks together. They dropped their sticks in when Rabbit said 'Go!' and then they had hurried across to the other side of the bridge, and now they were all leaning over the edge, waiting to see whose stick would come out first. But it was a long time coming, because the river was very lazy that day, and hardly seemed to mind if it didn't ever get there at all.

'I can see mine!' cried Roo. 'No, I can't, it's something else. Can you see yours, Piglet? I thought I could see mine, but I couldn't. There it is! No, it isn't. Can you see yours, Pooh?'

'No,' said Pooh.

'I expect my stick's stuck,' said Roo. 'Rabbit, my stick's stuck. Is your stick stuck, Piglet?'

'They always take longer than you think,' said Rabbit.

'How long do you *think* they'll take?' asked Roo.

'I can see yours, Piglet,' said Pooh suddenly.

'Mine's a sort of greyish one,' said Piglet, not daring to lean too far over in case he fell in.

'Yes, that's what I can see. It's coming over on to my side.'

Rabbit leant over further than ever, looking for his and Roo wriggled up and down, calling out 'Come on, stick! Stick, stick, stick!' and Piglet got very excited because his was the only one which had been seen, and that meant that he was winning.

'It's coming!' said Pooh.

'Are you *sure* it's mine?' squeaked Piglet excitedly.

'Yes, because it's grey. A big grey one. Here it comes!
A very – big – grey – Oh, no, it isn't, it's Eeyore.'

And out floated Eeyore.

'Eeyore!' cried everybody.

Looking very calm, very dignified, with his legs in the air, came Eeyore from beneath the bridge.

'It's Eeyore!' cried Roo, terribly excited.

'Is that so?' said Eeyore, getting caught up by a little eddy, and turning slowly round three times. 'I wondered.'

'I didn't know you were playing,' said Roo.

'I'm not,' said Eeyore.

'Eeyore, what *are* you doing there?' said Rabbit.

'I'll give you three guesses, Rabbit. Digging holes in the ground? Wrong. Leaping from branch to branch of a young oak-tree? Wrong. Waiting for somebody to help me out of the river? Right. Give Rabbit time, and he'll always get the answer.'

'But Eeyore,' said Pooh in distress, 'what can we –

I mean, how shall we – do you think if we –'

'Yes,' said Eeyore. 'One of those would be just the thing. Thank you, Pooh.'

'He's going *round* and *round*,' said Roo, much impressed.

'And why not?' said Eeyore coldly.

'I can swim too,' said Roo proudly.

'Not round and round,' said Eeyore. 'It's much more difficult. I didn't want to come swimming at all to-day,' he went on, revolving slowly. 'But if, when in, I decide to practise a slight circular movement from right to left – or perhaps I should say,' he added, as he got into another eddy, 'from left to right, just as it happens to occur to me, it is nobody's business but my own.'

There was a moment's silence while everybody thought.

'I've got a sort of idea,' said Pooh at last, 'but I don't suppose it's a very good one.'

'I don't suppose it is either,' said Eeyore.

'Go on, Pooh,' said Rabbit. 'Let's have it.'

'Well, if we all threw stones and things into the river on *one* side of Eeyore, the stones would make waves, and the waves would wash him to the other side.'

'That's a very good idea,' said Rabbit, and Pooh looked happy again.

'Very,' said Eeyore. 'When I want to be washed, Pooh, I'll let you know.'

'Supposing we hit him by mistake?' said Piglet anxiously.

'Or supposing you missed him by mistake,' said Eeyore. 'Think of all the possibilities, Piglet, before you settle down to enjoy yourselves.'

But Pooh had got the biggest stone he could carry, and was leaning over the bridge, holding it in his paws.

'I'm not throwing it, I'm dropping it, Eeyore,'

he explained. 'And then I can't miss – I mean I can't hit you. *Could* you stop turning round for a moment, because it muddles me rather?'

'No,' said Eeyore. 'I *like* turning round.'

Rabbit began to feel that it was time he took command.

'Now, Pooh,' he said, 'when I say "Now!" you can drop it. Eeyore, when I say "Now!" Pooh will drop his stone.'

'Thank you very much, Rabbit, but I expect I shall know.'

'Are you ready, Pooh? Piglet, give Pooh a little more room. Get back a bit there, Roo. Are you ready?'

'No,' said Eeyore.

'*Now!*' said Rabbit.

Pooh dropped his stone. There was a loud splash, and Eeyore disappeared . . .

It was an anxious moment for the watchers on the bridge. They looked and looked . . . and even the sight of Piglet's stick coming out a little in front of Rabbit's didn't cheer them up as much as you would have expected. And then, just as Pooh was beginning to think that he must have chosen the wrong stone or the wrong river or the wrong day for his Idea, something grey showed for a moment by the river bank . . . and it got slowly bigger and bigger . . . and at last it was Eeyore coming out.

With a shout they rushed off the bridge, and pushed and pulled at him; and soon he was standing among them again on dry land.

'Oh, Eeyore, you are wet!' said Piglet, feeling him.

Eeyore shook himself, and asked somebody to explain to Piglet what happened when you had been inside a river for quite a long time.

'Well done, Pooh,' said Rabbit kindly. 'That was a good idea of ours.'

'What was?' asked Eeyore.

'Hooshing you to the bank like that.'

'*Hooshing* me?' said Eeyore in surprise. 'Hooshing *me*? You didn't think I was *hooshed*, did you? I dived. Pooh dropped a large stone on me, and so as not to be struck heavily on the chest, I dived and swam to the bank.'

'You didn't really,' whispered Piglet to Pooh, so as to comfort him.

'I didn't *think* I did,' said Pooh anxiously.

'It's just Eeyore,' said Piglet. '*I* thought your Idea was a very good Idea.'

Pooh began to feel a little more comfortable, because when you are a Bear of Very Little Brain, and you Think of Things, you find sometimes that a Thing which seemed very Thingish inside you is quite different when it gets out into the open and has other people looking at it. And, anyhow, Eeyore *was* in the river, and now he *wasn't*, so he hadn't done any harm.

'How did you fall in, Eeyore?' asked Rabbit, as he dried him with Piglet's handkerchief.

'I didn't,' said Eeyore.

'But how –'

'I was BOUNCED,' said Eeyore.

'Oo,' said Roo excitedly, 'did somebody push you?'

'Somebody BOUNCED me. I was just thinking by the side of the river – thinking, if any of you know what that means – when I received a loud BOUNCE.'

'Oh, Eeyore!' said everybody.

'Are you sure you didn't slip?' asked Rabbit wisely.

'Of course I slipped. If you're standing on the slippery bank of a river, and somebody BOUNCES you loudly from behind, you slip. What did you think I did?'

'But who did it?' asked Roo.

Eeyore didn't answer.

'I expect it was Tigger,' said Piglet nervously.

'But, Eeyore,' said Pooh, 'was it a Joke, or an Accident? I mean –'

'I didn't stop to ask, Pooh. Even at the very bottom of the river I didn't stop to say to myself, "Is this a Hearty Joke, or is it the Merest Accident?" I just floated to the surface, and said to myself, "It's wet." If you know what I mean.'

'And where was Tigger?' asked Rabbit.

Before Eeyore could answer, there was a loud noise behind them, and through the hedge came Tigger himself.

'Hallo, everybody,' said Tigger cheerfully.

'Hallo, Tigger,' said Roo.

Rabbit became very important suddenly.

'Tigger,' he said solemnly, 'what happened just now?'

'Just when?' said Tigger a little uncomfortably.

'When you bounced Eeyore into the river.'

'I didn't bounce him.'

'You bounced me,' said Eeyore gruffly.

'I didn't really. I had a cough, and I happened to be behind Eeyore, and I said, "*Grrrr–oppp–ptschschschz.*"'

'Why?' said Rabbit, helping Piglet up, and dusting him. 'It's all right, Piglet.'

'It took me by surprise,' said Piglet nervously.

'That's what I call bouncing,' said Eeyore. 'Taking people by surprise. Very unpleasant habit. I don't mind Tigger being in the Forest,' he went on, 'because it's a large Forest, and there's plenty of room to bounce in it. But I don't see why he should come into *my* little corner of it, and bounce there. It isn't as if there was anything very wonderful about my little corner. Of course for people who like cold, wet, ugly bits it is something rather special, but otherwise it's just a corner, and if anybody feels bouncy –'

'I didn't bounce, I coughed,' said Tigger crossly.

'Bouncy or coffy, it's all the same at the bottom of the river.'

'Well,' said Rabbit, 'all I can say is – well, here's Christopher Robin, so *he* can say it.'

Christopher Robin came down from the Forest to the bridge, feeling all sunny and careless, and just as if twice nineteen didn't matter a bit, as it didn't on such a happy afternoon, and he thought that if he stood on the bottom rail of the bridge, and leant over, and watched the river slipping slowly away beneath him, then he would suddenly know everything that there was to be known, and he would be able to tell Pooh, who wasn't quite sure about some of it. But when he got to the bridge and saw all the animals there, then he knew that it

wasn't that kind of afternoon, but the other kind, when you wanted to *do* something.

'It's like this, Christopher Robin,' began Rabbit. 'Tigger –'

'No, I didn't,' said Tigger.

'Well, anyhow, there I was,' said Eeyore.

'But I don't think he meant to,' said Pooh.

'He just *is* bouncy,' said Piglet, 'and he can't help it.'

'Try bouncing *me*, Tigger,' said Roo eagerly. 'Eeyore, Tigger's going to try *me*. Piglet, do you think –'

'Yes, yes,' said Rabbit, 'we don't all want to speak at once. The point is, what does Christopher Robin think about it?'

'All I did was I coughed,' said Tigger.

'He bounced,' said Eeyore.

'Well, I sort of boffed,' said Tigger.

'Hush!' said Rabbit, holding up his paw. 'What does Christopher Robin think about it all? That's the point.'

'Well,' said Christopher Robin, not quite sure what it was all about. '*I* think –'

'Yes?' said everybody.

'*I* think we all ought to play Poohsticks.'

So they did. And Eeyore, who had never played it before, won more times than anybody else; and Roo fell in twice, the first time by accident and the second time on purpose, because he suddenly saw Kanga coming from the Forest, and he knew he'd have to go to bed anyhow. So then Rabbit said he'd go with them; and Tigger and Eeyore went off together, because Eeyore wanted to tell Tigger How to Win at Poohsticks, which you do by letting your stick drop in a twitchy sort of way, if you understand what I mean, Tigger; and Christopher Robin and Pooh and Piglet were left on the bridge by themselves.

For a long time they looked at the river beneath them, saying nothing, and the river said nothing too, for it felt

very quiet and peaceful on this summer afternoon.

'Tigger is all right, *really*,' said Piglet lazily.

'Of course he is,' said Christopher Robin.

'Everybody is *really*,' said Pooh. 'That's what *I* think,' said Pooh. 'But I don't suppose I'm right,' he said.

'Of course you are,' said Christopher Robin.

CHAPTER SEVEN

in which Tigger is unbounced

ONE DAY RABBIT AND PIGLET were sitting outside Pooh's front door listening to Rabbit, and Pooh was sitting with them. It was a drowsy summer afternoon, and the Forest was full of gentle sounds, which all seemed to be saying to Pooh, 'Don't listen to Rabbit, listen to me.' So he got into a comfortable position for not listening to Rabbit, and from time to time he opened his eyes to say 'Ah!' and then closed them again to say 'True,' and from time to time Rabbit said, 'You see what I mean, Piglet,' very earnestly, and Piglet nodded earnestly to show that he did.

'In fact,' said Rabbit, coming to the end of it at last, 'Tigger's getting so Bouncy nowadays that it's time we taught him a lesson. Don't you think so, Piglet?'

Piglet said that Tigger *was* very Bouncy, and that if they could think of a way of unbouncing him it would be a Very Good Idea.

'Just what I feel,' said Rabbit. 'What do *you* say, Pooh?'

Pooh opened his eyes with a jerk and said, 'Extremely.'

'Extremely what?' asked Rabbit.

'What you were saying,' said Pooh. 'Undoubtably.'

Piglet gave Pooh a stiffening sort of nudge, and Pooh,

who felt more and more that he was somewhere else, got up slowly and began to look for himself.

'But how shall we do it?' asked Piglet. 'What sort of a lesson, Rabbit?'

'That's the point,' said Rabbit.

The word 'lesson' came back to Pooh as one he had heard before somewhere.

'There's a thing called Twy-stymes,' he said. 'Christopher Robin tried to teach it to me once, but it didn't.'

'What didn't?' said Rabbit.

'Didn't what?' said Piglet.

Pooh shook his head.

'I don't know,' he said. 'It just didn't. What are we talking about?'

'Pooh,' said Piglet reproachfully, 'haven't you been listening to what Rabbit was saying?'

'I listened, but I had a small piece of fluff in my ear. Could you say it again, please, Rabbit?'

Rabbit never minded saying things again, so he asked where he should begin from; and when Pooh had said from the moment when the fluff got in his ear, and Rabbit had asked when that was, and Pooh had said he didn't know because he hadn't heard properly, Piglet settled it all by saying that what they were trying to do was, they were just trying to think of a way to get the bounces out of Tigger, because however much you liked him, you couldn't deny it, he *did* bounce.

'Oh, I see,' said Pooh.

'There's too much of him,' said Rabbit, 'that's what it comes to.'

Pooh tried to think, and all he could think of was

something which didn't help at all. So he hummed it very quietly to himself.

If Rabbit
Was bigger
And fatter
And stronger,
Or bigger
Than Tigger,
If Tigger was smaller,
Then Tigger's bad habit
Of bouncing at Rabbit
Would matter
No longer,
If Rabbit
Was taller.

'What was Pooh saying?' asked Rabbit. 'Any good?'

'No,' said Pooh sadly. 'No good.'

'Well, I've got an idea,' said Rabbit, 'and here it is. We take Tigger for a long explore, somewhere where he's never been, and we lose him there, and next morning we find him again, and – mark my words – he'll be a different Tigger altogether.'

'Why?' said Pooh.

'Because he'll be a Humble Tigger. Because he'll be a Sad Tigger, a Melancholy Tigger, a Small and Sorry

Tigger, an Oh-Rabbit-I-*am*-glad-to-see-you Tigger. That's why.'

'Will he be glad to see me and Piglet, too?'

'Of course.'

'That's good,' said Pooh.

'I should hate him to go *on* being Sad,' said Piglet doubtfully.

'Tiggers never go on being Sad,' explained Rabbit. 'They get over it with Astonishing Rapidity. I asked Owl, just to make sure, and he said that that's what they always get over it with. But if we can make Tigger feel Small and Sad just for five minutes, we shall have done a good deed.'

'Would Christopher Robin think so?' asked Piglet.

'Yes,' said Rabbit. 'He'd say, "You've done a good deed, Piglet. I would have done it myself, only I happened to be doing something else. Thank you, Piglet." And Pooh, of course.'

Piglet felt very glad about this, and he saw at once that what they were going to do to Tigger was a good thing to do, and as Pooh and Rabbit were doing it with him, it was a thing which even a Very Small Animal could wake up in the morning and be comfortable about doing. So the only question was, where should they lose Tigger?

'We'll take him to the North Pole,' said Rabbit,

'because it was a very long explore finding it, so it will be a very long explore for Tigger un-finding it again.'

It was now Pooh's turn to feel very glad, because it was he who had first found the North Pole, and when they got there, Tigger would see a notice which said, 'Discovered by Pooh, Pooh found it,' and then Tigger would know, which perhaps he didn't now, the sort of Bear Pooh was. *That* sort of Bear.

So it was arranged that they should start next morning, and that Rabbit, who lived near Kanga and Roo and Tigger, should now go home and ask Tigger what he was doing to-morrow, because if he wasn't doing anything, what about coming for an explore and getting Pooh and Piglet to come too? And if Tigger said 'Yes' that would be all right, and if he said 'No' –

'He won't,' said Rabbit. 'Leave it to me.' And he went off busily.

The next day was quite a different day. Instead of being hot and sunny, it was cold and misty. Pooh didn't mind for himself, but when he thought of all the honey the bees wouldn't be making, a cold and misty day always made him feel sorry for them. He said so to Piglet when Piglet came to fetch him, and Piglet said that he wasn't thinking of that so much, but of how cold and miserable it would be being lost all day and night on the top of the Forest.

But when he and Pooh had got to Rabbit's house, Rabbit said it was just the day for them, because Tigger always bounced on ahead of everybody, and as soon as he got out of sight, they would hurry away in the other direction, and he would never see them again.

'Not never?' said Piglet.

'Well, not until we find him again, Piglet. To-morrow, or whenever it is. Come on. He's waiting for us.'

When they got to Kanga's house, they found that Roo was waiting too, being a great friend of Tigger's, which made it Awkward; but Rabbit whispered, 'Leave this to me,' behind his paw to Pooh, and went up to Kanga.

'I don't think Roo had better come,' he said. 'Not to-day.'

'Why not?' said Roo, who wasn't supposed to be listening.

'Nasty cold day,' said Rabbit, shaking his head. 'And you were coughing this morning.'

'How do you know?' asked Roo indignantly.

'Oh, Roo, you never told me,' said Kanga reproachfully.

'It was a biscuit cough,' said Roo, 'not one you tell about.'

'I think not to-day, dear. Another day.'

'To-morrow?' said Roo hopefully.

'We'll see,' said Kanga.

'You're always seeing, and nothing ever happens,' said Roo sadly.

'Nobody could see on a day like this, Roo,' said Rabbit. 'I don't expect we shall get very far, and then this afternoon we'll all – we'll all – we'll – ah, Tigger, there you are. Come on. Good-bye, Roo! This afternoon we'll – come on, Pooh! All ready? That's right. Come on.'

So they went. At first Pooh and Rabbit and Piglet walked together, and Tigger ran round them in circles, and then, when the path got narrower, Rabbit, Piglet and Pooh walked one after another, and Tigger ran round them in oblongs, and by-and-by, when the gorse got very prickly on each side of the path, Tigger ran up and down in front of them, and sometimes he bounced into Rabbit and sometimes he didn't. And as they got higher, the mist got thicker, so

that Tigger kept disappearing, and then when you thought he wasn't there, there he was again, saying, 'I say, come on,' and before you could say anything, there he wasn't.

Rabbit turned round and nudged Piglet.

'The next time,' he said. 'Tell Pooh.'

'The next time,' said Piglet to Pooh.

'The next what?' said Pooh to Piglet.

Tigger appeared suddenly, bounced into Rabbit, and disappeared again. 'Now!' said Rabbit. He jumped into a hollow by the side of the path, and Pooh and Piglet jumped after him. They crouched in the bracken, listening. The Forest was very silent when you stopped and listened to it. They could see nothing and hear nothing.

'H'sh!' said Rabbit.

'I am,' said Pooh.

There was a pattering noise . . . then silence again.

'Hallo!' said Tigger, and he sounded so close suddenly that Piglet would have jumped if Pooh hadn't accidentally been sitting on most of him.

'Where are you?' called Tigger.

Rabbit nudged Pooh, and Pooh looked about for Piglet to nudge, but couldn't find him, and Piglet went on breathing wet bracken as quietly as he could, and felt very brave and excited.

'That's funny,' said Tigger.

There was a moment's silence, and then they heard him pattering off again. For a little longer they waited, until the Forest had become so still that it almost frightened them, and then Rabbit got up and stretched himself.

'Well?' he whispered proudly. 'There we are! Just as I said.'

'I've been thinking,' said Pooh, 'and I think –'

'No,' said Rabbit. 'Don't. Run. Come on.' And they all hurried off, Rabbit leading the way.

'Now,' said Rabbit, after they had gone a little way, 'we can talk. What were you going to say, Pooh?'

'Nothing much. Why are we going along here?'

'Because it's the way home.'

'Oh!' said Pooh.

'I *think* it's more to the right,' said Piglet nervously. 'What do *you* think, Pooh?'

Pooh looked at his two paws. He knew that one of them was the

right, and he knew that when you had decided which one of them was the right, then the other one was the left, but he never could remember how to begin.

'Well –' he said slowly.

'Come on,' said Rabbit. 'I know it's this way.'

They went on. Ten minutes later they stopped again.

'It's very silly,' said Rabbit, 'but just for the moment I – Ah, of course. Come on.' . . .

'Here we are,' said Rabbit ten minutes later. 'No, we're not.' . . .

'Now,' said Rabbit ten minutes later, 'I think we ought to be getting – or  are we a little bit more to the right than I thought?' . . .

'It's a funny thing,' said Rabbit ten minutes later, 'how everything looks the same in a mist. Have you noticed it, Pooh?'

Pooh said that he had.

'Lucky we know the Forest so well, or we might get lost,' said Rabbit half an hour later, and he gave the careless laugh which you give when you know the Forest so well that you can't get lost.

Piglet sidled up to Pooh from behind.

'Pooh!' he whispered.

'Yes, Piglet?'

'Nothing,' said Piglet, taking Pooh's paw. 'I just wanted to be sure of you.'

＊　＊　＊

When Tigger had finished waiting for the others to catch him up, and they hadn't, and when he had got tired of having nobody to say, 'I say, come on' to, he thought he would go home. So he trotted back; and the first thing Kanga said when she saw him was, 'There's a good Tigger. You're just in time for your Strengthening Medicine,' and she poured it out for him. Roo said proudly, 'I've *had* mine,' and Tigger swallowed his and said, 'So have I,' and then he and Roo pushed each other about in a friendly way, and Tigger accidentally knocked over one or two chairs by accident, and Roo accidentally knocked over one on purpose, and Kanga said, 'Now then, run along.'

'Where shall we run along to?' asked Roo.

'You can go and collect some fir-cones for me,' said Kanga, giving them a basket.

So they went to the Six Pine Trees, and threw fir-cones

at each other until they had forgotten what they came for, and they left the basket under the trees and went back to dinner. And it was just as they were finishing dinner that Christopher Robin put his head in at the door.

'Where's Pooh?' he asked.

'Tigger dear, where's Pooh?' said Kanga. Tigger explained what had happened at the same time that Roo was explaining about his Biscuit Cough and Kanga was telling them not both to talk at once, so it was some time before Christopher Robin guessed that Pooh and Piglet and Rabbit were all lost in the mist on the top of the Forest.

'It's a funny thing about Tiggers,' whispered Tigger to Roo, 'how Tiggers *never* get lost.'

'Why don't they, Tigger?'

'They just don't,' explained Tigger. 'That's how it is.'

'Well,' said Christopher Robin, 'we shall have to go and find them, that's all. Come on, Tigger.'

'I shall have to go and find them,' explained Tigger to Roo.

'May I find them too?' asked Roo eagerly.

'I think not to-day, dear,' said Kanga. 'Another day.'

'Well, if they're lost to-morrow, may I find them?'

'We'll see,' said Kanga, and Roo, who knew what *that* meant, went into a corner and practised jumping out at himself, partly because he wanted to practise this, and partly because he didn't want Christopher Robin and Tigger to think that he minded when they went off without him.

＊　＊　＊

'The fact is,' said Rabbit, 'we've missed our way somehow.'

They were having a rest in a small sand-pit on the top of the Forest. Pooh was getting rather tired of that sand-pit, and suspected it of following them about, because whichever direction they started in, they always ended up at it, and each time, as it came through the mist at them, Rabbit said triumphantly, 'Now I know where we are!' and Pooh said sadly, 'So do I,' and Piglet said nothing. He had tried to think of something to say, but the only thing he could think of was, 'Help, help!' and it seemed silly to say that, when he had Pooh and Rabbit with him.

'Well,' said Rabbit, after a long silence in which nobody

thanked him for the nice walk they were having, 'we'd better get on, I suppose. Which way shall we try?'

'How would it be,' said Pooh slowly, 'if, as soon as we're out of sight of this Pit, we try to find it again?'

'What's the good of that?' said Rabbit.

'Well,' said Pooh, 'we keep looking for Home and not finding it, so I thought that if we looked for this Pit, we'd be sure not to find it, which would be a Good Thing, because then we might find something that we *weren't* looking for, which might be just what we *were* looking for, really.'

'I don't see much sense in that,' said Rabbit.

'No,' said Pooh humbly, 'there isn't. But there was *going* to be when I began it. It's just that something happened to it on the way.'

'If I walked away from this Pit, and then walked back to it, of *course* I should find it.'

'Well, I thought perhaps you wouldn't,' said Pooh. 'I just thought.'

'Try,' said Piglet suddenly. 'We'll wait here for you.'

Rabbit gave a laugh to show how silly Piglet was, and walked into the mist. After he had gone a hundred yards, he turned and walked back again . . . and after Pooh and Piglet had waited twenty minutes for him, Pooh got up.

'I just thought,' said Pooh. 'Now then, Piglet, let's go home.'

'But, Pooh,' cried Piglet, all excited, 'do you know the way?'

'No,' said Pooh. 'But there are twelve pots of honey in my cupboard, and they've been calling to me for hours. I couldn't hear them properly before because Rabbit *would* talk, but if nobody says anything except those twelve pots, I *think*, Piglet, I shall know where they're coming from. Come on.'

They walked off together; and for a long time Piglet said nothing, so as not to interrupt the pots; and then suddenly he made a squeaky noise . . . and an oo-noise . . . because now he began to know where he was; but he still didn't dare to say so out loud, in case he wasn't. And just when he was getting so sure of himself that it didn't matter whether the pots went on calling or not, there was a shout from in front of them, and out of the mist came Christopher Robin.

'Oh, there you are,' said Christopher Robin carelessly, trying to pretend that he hadn't been anxious.

'Here we are,' said Pooh.

'Where's Rabbit?'

'I don't know,' said Pooh.

'Oh – well, I expect Tigger will find him. He's sort of looking for you all.'

'Well,' said Pooh, 'I've got to go home for something, and so has Piglet, because we haven't had it yet, and –'

'I'll come and watch you,' said Christopher Robin.

So he went home with Pooh, and watched him for quite a long time . . . and all the time he was watching, Tigger was tearing round the Forest making loud yapping noises for Rabbit. And at last a very Small and Sorry Rabbit heard him. And the Small and Sorry Rabbit rushed through the mist at the noise, and it suddenly turned into Tigger; a Friendly Tigger, a Grand

Tigger, a Large and Helpful Tigger, a Tigger who bounced, if he bounced at all, in just the beautiful way a Tigger ought to bounce.

'Oh, Tigger, I *am* glad to see you,' cried Rabbit.

CHAPTER EIGHT

in which Piglet
does a Very Grand Thing

HALF-WAY BETWEEN POOH'S HOUSE and Piglet's house was a Thoughtful Spot where they met sometimes when they had decided to go and see each other, and as it was warm and out of the wind they would sit down there for a little and wonder what they would do now that they *had* seen each other. One day when they had decided not to do anything, Pooh made up a verse about it, so that everybody should know what the place was for.

> This warm and sunny Spot
> Belongs to Pooh.
> And here he wonders what
> He's going to do.
> Oh, bother, I forgot –
> It's Piglet's too.

Now one autumn morning when the wind had blown all the leaves off the trees in the night, and was trying to blow the branches off, Pooh and Piglet were sitting in the Thoughtful Spot and wondering.

'What *I* think,' said Pooh, 'is I think we'll go to Pooh Corner and see Eeyore, because perhaps his house has been blown down, and perhaps he'd like us to build it again.'

'What *I* think,' said Piglet, 'is I think we'll go and see Christopher Robin, only he won't be there, so we can't.'

'Let's go and see *everybody*,' said Pooh. 'Because when you've been walking in the wind for miles, and you suddenly go into somebody's house, and he says, "Hallo, Pooh, you're just in time for a little smackerel of something," and you are, then it's what I call a Friendly Day.'

Piglet thought that they ought to have a Reason for going to see everybody, like Looking for Small or Organizing an Expotition, if Pooh could think of something.

Pooh could.

'We'll go because it's Thursday,' he said, 'and we'll go to wish everybody a Very Happy Thursday. Come on, Piglet.'

They got up; and when Piglet had sat down again,

because he didn't know the wind was so strong, and had been helped up by Pooh, they started off. They went to Pooh's house first, and luckily Pooh was at home just as they got there, so he asked them in, and they had some, and then they went on to Kanga's house, holding on to each other, and shouting, 'Isn't it?' and 'What?' and 'I can't hear.' By the time they got to Kanga's house they were so buffeted that they stayed to lunch. Just at

first it seemed rather cold outside afterwards, so they pushed on to Rabbit's as quickly as they could.

'We've come to wish you a Very Happy Thursday,' said Pooh, when he had gone in and out once or twice just to make sure that he *could* get out again.

'Why, what's going to happen on Thursday?' asked Rabbit, and when Pooh had explained, and Rabbit, whose life was made up of Important Things, said, 'Oh, I thought you'd really come about something,' they sat down for a little . . . and by-and-by Pooh and Piglet went on again. The wind was behind them now, so they didn't have to shout.

'Rabbit's clever,' said Pooh thoughtfully.

'Yes,' said Piglet, 'Rabbit's clever.'

'And he has Brain.'

'Yes,' said Piglet, 'Rabbit has Brain.'

There was a long silence.

'I suppose,' said Pooh, 'that that's why he never understands anything.'

Christopher Robin was at home by this time, because it was the afternoon, and he was so glad to see them that they stayed there until very nearly tea-time, and then they had a Very Nearly tea, which is one you forget about afterwards, and hurried on to Pooh Corner, so as to see Eeyore before it was too late to have a Proper Tea with Owl.

'Hallo, Eeyore,' they called out cheerfully.

'Ah!' said Eeyore. 'Lost your way?'

'We just came to see you,' said Piglet. 'And to see how your house was. Look, Pooh, it's still standing!'

'I know,' said Eeyore. 'Very odd. Somebody ought to have come down and pushed it over.'

'We wondered whether the wind would blow it down,' said Pooh.

'Ah, that's why nobody's bothered, I suppose. I thought perhaps they'd forgotten.'

'Well, we're very glad to see you, Eeyore, and now we're going on to see Owl.'

'That's right. You'll like Owl. He flew past a day or two ago and noticed me. He didn't actually say anything, mind you, but he knew it was me. Very friendly of him, I thought. Encouraging.'

Pooh and Piglet shuffled about a little and said, 'Well, good-bye, Eeyore,' as lingeringly as they could, but they had a long way to go, and wanted to be getting on.

'Good-bye,' said Eeyore. 'Mind you don't get blown away, little Piglet. You'd be missed. People would say, "Where's little Piglet been blown to?" – really wanting to know. Well, good-bye. And thank you for happening to pass me.'

'Good-bye,' said Pooh and Piglet for the last time, and they pushed on to Owl's house.

The wind was against them now, and Piglet's ears

 streamed behind him

like banners

 as he fought his way along,

and it seemed hours before he got them into the shelter of the Hundred Acre Wood and they stood up straight again, to listen, a little nervously, to the roaring of the gale among the tree-tops.

'Supposing a tree fell down, Pooh, when we were underneath it?'

'Supposing it didn't,' said Pooh after careful thought.

Piglet was comforted by this, and in a little while they were knocking and ringing very cheerfully at Owl's door.

'Hallo, Owl,' said Pooh. 'I hope we're not too late for – I mean, how are you, Owl? Piglet and I just came to see how you were because it's Thursday.'

'Sit down, Pooh, sit down, Piglet,' said Owl kindly. 'Make yourselves comfortable.'

They thanked him, and made themselves as comfortable as they could.

'Because, you see, Owl,' said Pooh, 'we've been hurrying, so as to be in time for – so as to see you before we went away again.'

Owl nodded solemnly.

'Correct me if I am wrong,' he said, 'but am I right in supposing that it is a very Blusterous day outside?'

'Very,' said Piglet, who was quietly thawing his ears, and wishing that he was safely back in his own house.

'I thought so,' said Owl. 'It was on just such a

blusterous day as this that my Uncle Robert, a portrait of whom you see upon the wall on your right, Piglet, while returning in the late forenoon from a – What's that?'

There was a loud cracking noise.

'Look out!' cried Pooh. 'Mind the clock! Out of the way, Piglet! Piglet, I'm falling on you!'

'Help!' cried Piglet.

Pooh's side of the room was slowly tilting upwards and his chair began sliding down on Piglet's. The clock slithered gently along the mantelpiece, collecting vases on the way, until they all crashed together on to what had once been the floor, but was now trying to see what it looked like as a wall. Uncle Robert, who was going to be the new hearthrug, and was bringing the rest of his wall with him as carpet, met Piglet's chair just as Piglet was expecting to leave it, and for a little while it became very difficult to remember which was really the north. Then there was another loud crack . . . Owl's room collected itself feverishly . . . and there was silence.

* * *

In a corner of the room,
the table-cloth began
to wriggle.

Then it wrapped itself
into a ball and rolled
across the room.

Then it jumped up
and down once or twice,

and put out two ears.

It rolled across the room
again, and unwound itself.

'Pooh,' said Piglet nervously.

'Yes,' said one of the chairs.

'Where are we?'

'I'm not quite sure,' said the chair.

'Are we – are we in Owl's House?'

'I think so, because we were just going to have tea, and we hadn't had it.'

'Oh!' said Piglet. 'Well, did Owl *always* have a letter-box in his ceiling?'

'Has he?'

'Yes, look.'

'I can't,' said Pooh. 'I'm face downwards under something, and that, Piglet, is a very bad position for looking at ceilings.'

'Well, he has, Pooh.'

'Perhaps he's changed it,' said Pooh. 'Just for a change.'

There was a disturbance behind the table in the other corner of the room, and Owl was with them again.

'Ah, Piglet,' said Owl, looking very much annoyed; 'where's Pooh?'

'I'm not quite sure,' said Pooh.

Owl turned at his voice, and frowned at as much of Pooh as he could see.

'Pooh,' said Owl severely, 'did *you* do that?'

'No,' said Pooh humbly. 'I don't *think* so.'

'Then who did?'

'I think it was the wind,' said Piglet. 'I think your house has blown down.'

'Oh, is that it? I thought it was Pooh.'

'No,' said Pooh.

'If it was the wind,' said Owl, considering the matter, 'then it wasn't Pooh's fault. No blame can be attached to him.' With these kind words he flew up to look at his new ceiling.

'Piglet!' called Pooh in a loud whisper.

Piglet leant down to him.

'Yes, Pooh?'

'*What* did he say was attached to me?'

'He said he didn't blame you.'

'Oh! I thought he meant – Oh, I see.'

'Owl,' said Piglet, 'come down and help Pooh.'

Owl, who was admiring his letter-box, flew down again. Together they pushed and pulled at the armchair, and in a little while Pooh came out from underneath, and was able to look round him again.

'Well!' said Owl. 'This is a nice state of things!'

'What are we going to do, Pooh? Can you think of anything?' asked Piglet.

'Well, I *had* just thought of something,' said Pooh. 'It was just a little thing I thought of.' And he began to sing:

I lay on my chest
And I thought it best
To pretend I was having an evening rest;
I lay on my tum
And I tried to hum
But nothing particular seemed to come.
My face was flat
On the floor, and that
Is all very well for an acrobat;
But it doesn't seem fair
To a Friendly Bear
To stiffen him out with a basket-chair.
And a sort of sqoze
Which grows and grows
Is not too nice for his poor old nose,
And a sort of squch
Is much too much
For his neck and his mouth and his ears and such.

'That was all,' said Pooh.

Owl coughed in an unadmiring sort of way, and said

that, if Pooh was sure that *was* all, they could now give their minds to the Problem of Escape.

'Because,' said Owl, 'we can't go out by what used to be the front door. Something's fallen on it.'

'But how else *can* you go out?' asked Piglet anxiously.

'That is the Problem, Piglet, to which I am asking Pooh to give his mind.'

Pooh sat on the floor which had once been a wall, and gazed up at the ceiling which had once been another wall, with a front door in it which had once been a front door, and tried to give his mind to it.

'Could you fly up to the letter-box with Piglet on your back?' he asked.

'No,' said Piglet quickly. 'He couldn't.'

Owl explained about the Necessary Dorsal Muscles. He had explained this to Pooh and Christopher Robin once before, and had been waiting ever since for a chance to do it again, because it is a thing which you can easily explain twice before anybody knows what you are talking about.

'Because you see, Owl, if we could get Piglet into the letter-box, he might squeeze through the place where the letters come, and climb down the tree and run for help.'

Piglet said hurriedly that he had been getting bigger lately, and couldn't *possibly*, much as he would like to, and

Owl said that he had had his letter-box made bigger lately in case he got bigger letters, so perhaps Piglet *might*, and Piglet said, 'But you said the necessary you-know-whats *wouldn't*,' and Owl said, 'No, they *won't*, so it's no good thinking about it,' and Piglet said, 'Then we'd better think of something else,' and began to at once.

But Pooh's mind had gone back to the day when he had saved Piglet from the flood, and everybody had admired him so much; and as that didn't often happen, he thought he would like it to happen again. And suddenly, just as it had come before, an idea came to him.

'Owl,' said Pooh, 'I have thought of something.'

'Astute and Helpful Bear,' said Owl.

Pooh looked proud at being called a stout and helpful bear, and said modestly that he just happened to think of it. You tied a piece of string to Piglet, and you flew up to the letter-box, with the other end in your beak, and you pushed it through the wire and brought it down to the floor, and you and Pooh pulled hard at this end, and Piglet went slowly up at the other end. And there you were.

'And there Piglet is,' said Owl. 'If the string doesn't break.'

'Supposing it does?' asked Piglet, really wanting to know.

'Then we try another piece of string.'

This was not very comforting to Piglet, because however many pieces of string they tried pulling up with, it would always be the same him coming down; but still, it did seem the only thing to do. So with one last look back in his mind at all the happy hours he had spent in the Forest *not* being pulled up to the ceiling by a piece of string, Piglet nodded bravely at Pooh and said that it was a Very Clever pup-pup-pup Clever pup-pup Plan.

'It won't break,' whispered Pooh comfortingly, 'because you're a Small Animal, and I'll stand underneath, and if you save us all, it will be a Very Grand Thing to talk about afterwards, and perhaps I'll make up a Song, and people will say, "It was so grand what Piglet did that a Respectful Pooh Song was made about it!"'

Piglet felt much better after this, and when everything was ready, and he found himself slowly going up to the ceiling, he was so proud that he would have called out 'Look at *me!*' if he hadn't been afraid that Pooh and Owl would let go of their end of the string and look at him.

'Up we go!' said Pooh cheerfully.

'The ascent is proceeding as expected,' said Owl helpfully. Soon it was over. Piglet opened the letter-box and climbed in. Then,

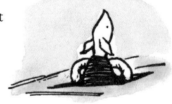

having untied himself, he began to squeeze into the slit, through which in the old days when front doors

were front doors, many an unexpected letter that WOL had written to himself, had come slipping.

He squeezed and he

sqoze, and then with one last squze he was out. Happy and excited he turned round to squeak a last message to the prisoners.

'It's all right,' he called through the letter-box. 'Your tree is blown right over, Owl, and there's a branch across the door, but Christopher Robin and I can move it, and we'll bring a rope for Pooh, and I'll go and tell him now, and I can climb down quite easily, I mean it's dangerous but I can do it all right, and Christopher Robin and I will be back in about half an hour. Good-bye, Pooh!' And without waiting to hear Pooh's answering 'Good-bye, and thank you, Piglet,' he was off.

'Half an hour,' said Owl, settling himself comfortably. 'That will just give me time to finish that story I was telling you about my Uncle Robert – a portrait of whom you see underneath you. Now let me see, where was I? Oh, yes. It was on just such a blusterous day as this that my Uncle Robert –'

Pooh closed his eyes.

CHAPTER NINE

in which Eeyore finds the Wolery
and Owl moves into it

Pooh had wandered into the Hundred Acre Wood, and was standing in front of what had once been Owl's House. It didn't look at all like a house now; it looked like a tree which had been blown down; and as soon as a house looks like that, it is time you tried to find another one. Pooh had had a Mysterious Missage underneath his front door that morning, saying, 'I AM SCERCHING FOR A NEW HOUSE FOR OWL SO HAD YOU RABBIT,' and while he was wondering what it meant Rabbit had come in and read it for him.

'I'm leaving one for all the others,' said Rabbit, 'and telling them what it means, and they'll all search too. I'm in a hurry, good-bye.' And he had run off.

Pooh followed slowly. He had something better to do than to find a new house for Owl; he had to make up a Pooh song about the old one. Because he had promised

Piglet days and days ago that he would, and whenever he and Piglet had met since, Piglet didn't actually say anything, but you knew at once why he didn't; and if anybody mentioned Hums or Trees or String or Storms-in-the-Night, Piglet's nose went all pink at the tip, and he talked about something quite different in a hurried sort of way.

'But it isn't Easy,' said Pooh to himself, as he looked at what had once been Owl's House. 'Because Poetry and Hums aren't things which you get, they're things which get *you*. And all you can do is to go where they can find you.'

He waited hopefully . . .

'Well,' said Pooh after a long wait, 'I shall begin *"Here lies a tree"* because it does, and then I'll see what happens.'

This is what happened:

> Here lies a tree which Owl (a bird)
>   Was fond of when it stood on end,
>   And Owl was talking to a friend
> Called Me (in case you hadn't heard)
> When something Oo occurred.
>
> For lo! the wind was blusterous
> And flattened out his favourite tree;
>   And things looked bad for him and we –
>   Looked bad, I mean, for he and us –
> I've never known them wuss.
>
> The Piglet (PIGLET) thought a thing:
>   'Courage!' he said. 'There's always hope.
>   I want a thinnish piece of rope.
> Or, if there isn't any, bring
> A thickish piece of string.'

So to the letter-box he rose,
  While Pooh and Owl said 'Oh!' and 'Hum!'
  And where the letters always come
(Called 'LETTERS ONLY') Piglet sqoze
His head and then his toes.

O gallant Piglet (PIGLET)! Ho!
  Did Piglet tremble? Did he blinch?
  No, no, he struggled inch by inch
Through LETTERS ONLY, as I know
Because I saw him go.

He ran and ran, and then he stood
  And shouted, 'Help for Owl, a bird,
  And Pooh, a bear!' until he heard
The others coming through the wood
As quickly as they could.

'Help-help and Rescue!' Piglet cried,
  And showed the others where to go.
  [Sing ho! for Piglet (PIGLET) ho!]
And soon the door was opened wide,
And we were both outside!

Sing ho! for Piglet, ho!
Ho!

'So there it is,' said Pooh, when he had sung this to himself three times. 'It's come different from what I thought it would, but it's come. Now I must go and sing it to Piglet.'

I AM SCERCHING FOR A NEW HOUSE FOR OWL SO HAD YOU RABBIT.

'What's all this?' said Eeyore.

Rabbit explained.

'What's the matter with his old house?'

Rabbit explained.

'Nobody tells me,' said Eeyore. 'Nobody keeps me informed. I make it seventeen days come Friday since anybody spoke to me.'

'It certainly isn't seventeen days –'

'Come Friday,' explained Eeyore.

'And today's Saturday,' said Rabbit. 'So that would make it eleven days. And I was here myself a week ago.'

'Not conversing,' said Eeyore. 'Not first one and then the other. You said "Hallo" and Flashed Past. I saw your tail a hundred yards up the hill as I was meditating my reply. I *had* thought of saying "What?" – but, of course, it was then too late.'

'Well, I was in a hurry.'

'No Give and Take,' Eeyore went on. 'No Exchange

of Thought. *"Hallo – What"* – I mean, it gets you nowhere, particularly if the other person's tail is only just in sight for the second half of the conversation.'

'It's your fault, Eeyore. You've never been to see any of us. You just stay here in this one corner of the Forest waiting for the others to come to *you*. Why don't you go to *them* sometimes?'

Eeyore was silent for a little while, thinking.

'There may be something in what you say, Rabbit,' he said at last. 'I have been neglecting you. I must move about more. I must come and go.'

'That's right, Eeyore. Drop in on any of us at any time, when you feel like it.'

'Thank-you, Rabbit. And if anybody says in a Loud Voice, "Bother, it's Eeyore," I can drop out again.'

Rabbit stood on one leg for a moment.

'Well,' he said, 'I must be going. I am rather busy this morning.'

'Good-bye,' said Eeyore.

'What? Oh, good-bye. And if you happen to come across a good house for Owl, you must let us know.'

'I will give my mind to it,' said Eeyore.

Rabbit went.

* * *

Pooh had found Piglet, and they were walking back to the Hundred Acre Wood together.

'Piglet,' said Pooh a little shyly, after they had walked for some time without saying anything.

'Yes, Pooh?'

'Do you remember when I said that a Respectful Pooh Song might be written about You Know What?'

'Did you, Pooh?' said Piglet, getting a little pink round the nose. 'Oh, yes, I believe you did.'

'It's been written, Piglet.'

The pink went slowly up Piglet's nose to his ears, and settled there.

'Has it, Pooh?' he asked huskily. 'About – about – That Time When? – Do you mean really written?'

'Yes, Piglet.'

The tips of Piglet's ears glowed suddenly, and he tried to say something; but even after he had husked once or twice, nothing came out. So Pooh went on:

'There are seven verses in it.'

'Seven?' said Piglet as carelessly as he could. 'You don't often get *seven* verses in a Hum, do you, Pooh?'

'Never,' said Pooh. 'I don't suppose it's *ever* been heard of before.'

'Do the Others know yet?' asked Piglet, stopping for a moment to pick up a stick and throw it away.

'No,' said Pooh. 'And I wondered which you would like best: for me to hum it now, or to wait till we find the others, and then hum it to all of you?'

Piglet thought for a little.

'I think what I'd like best, Pooh, is I'd like you to hum it to me *now* – and – and *then* to hum it to all of us. Because then Everybody would hear it, but I could say, "Oh, yes, Pooh's told me," and pretend not to be listening.'

So Pooh hummed it to him, all the seven verses, and Piglet said nothing, but just stood and glowed. For never before had anyone sung ho for Piglet (PIGLET) ho all by himself. When it was over, he wanted to ask for one of the verses over again, but didn't quite like to. It was the verse beginning 'O gallant Piglet,' and it seemed to him a very thoughtful way of beginning a piece of poetry.

'Did I really do all that?' he said at last.

'Well,' said Pooh, 'in poetry – in a piece of poetry – well, you *did* it, Piglet, because the poetry says you did. And that's how people know.'

'Oh!' said Piglet. 'Because I – I thought I did blinch a little. Just at first. And it says, "Did he blinch no no." That's why.'

'You only blinched inside,' said Pooh, 'and that's the bravest way for a Very Small Animal not to blinch that there is.'

Piglet sighed with happiness, and began to think about himself. He was BRAVE . . .

When they got to Owl's old house, they found everybody else there except Eeyore. Christopher Robin was telling them what to do, and Rabbit was telling them again directly afterwards, in case they hadn't heard, and then they were all doing it. They had got a rope and were pulling Owl's chairs and pictures and things out of his old house so as to be ready to put them into his new one.

Kanga was down below tying the things on, and calling out to Owl, 'You won't want this dirty old dish-cloth any more, will you, and what about this carpet, it's all in holes,' and Owl was calling back indignantly, 'Of course I do! It's just a question of arranging the furniture properly, and it isn't a dish-cloth, it's my shawl.' Every now and then Roo fell in and came back on the rope with the next article, which flustered Kanga a little because she never knew where to look for him. So she got cross with Owl and said that his house was a Disgrace, all damp and dirty, and it was quite time it did tumble down. Look at that horrid bunch of toadstools growing out of the corner there! So Owl looked down,

a little surprised because he didn't know about this, and then gave a short sarcastic laugh, and explained that this was his sponge, and that if people didn't know a perfectly ordinary bath-sponge when they saw it, things were coming to a pretty pass. '*Well!*' said Kanga, and Roo fell in quickly, crying, 'I *must* see Owl's sponge! Oh, there it is! Oh, Owl! Owl, it isn't a sponge, it's a spudge! Do you know what a spudge is, Owl? It's when your sponge gets all –' and Kanga said, 'Roo, dear!' very quickly, because that's *not* the way to talk to anybody who can spell TUESDAY.

But they were all quite happy when Pooh and Piglet came along, and they stopped working in order to have a little rest and listen to Pooh's new song. So then they all told Pooh how good it was, and Piglet said carelessly, 'It *is* good, isn't it? I mean as a song.'

'And what about the new house?' asked Pooh. 'Have you found it, Owl?'

'He's found a name for it,' said Christopher Robin, lazily nibbling at a piece of grass, 'so now all he wants is the house.'

'I am calling it this,' said Owl importantly, and he showed them what he had been making. It was a square piece of board with the name of the house painted on it:

THE WOLERY

It was at this exciting moment that something came through the trees, and bumped into Owl. The board fell to the ground, and Piglet and Roo bent over it eagerly.

'Oh, it's you,' said Owl crossly.

'Hallo, Eeyore!' said Rabbit. '*There* you are! Where have *you* been?'

Eeyore took no notice of them.

'Good morning, Christopher Robin,' he said, brushing away Roo and Piglet, and sitting down on THE WOLERY. 'Are we alone?'

'Yes,' said Christopher Robin, smiling to himself.

'I have been told – the news has worked through to my corner of the Forest – the damp bit down on the right which nobody wants – that a certain Person is looking for a house. I have found one for him.'

'Ah, well done,' said Rabbit kindly.

Eeyore looked round slowly at him, and then turned back to Christopher Robin.

'We have been joined by something,' he said in a loud whisper. 'But no matter. We can leave it behind. If you will come with me, Christopher Robin, I will show you the house.'

Christopher Robin jumped up.

'Come on, Pooh,' he said.

'Come on, Tigger!' cried Roo.

'Shall we go, Owl?' said Rabbit.

'Wait a moment,' said Owl, picking up his notice-board, which had just come into sight again.

Eeyore waved them back.

'Christopher Robin and I are going for a Short Walk,' he said, 'not a Jostle. If he likes to bring Pooh and Piglet with him, I shall be glad of their company, but one must be able to Breathe.'

'That's all right,' said Rabbit, rather glad to be left in charge of something. 'We'll go on getting the things out. Now then, Tigger, where's that rope? What's the matter, Owl?'

Owl, who had just discovered that his new address was THE SMEAR, coughed at Eeyore sternly, but said nothing, and Eeyore, with most of THE WOLERY behind him, marched off with his friends.

So, in a little while, they came to the house which Eeyore had found, and just before they came to it, Piglet

was nudging Pooh, and Pooh was nudging Piglet, and they were saying, 'It is!' and 'It can't be!' and 'It is, *really!'* to each other.

And when they got there, it really was.

'There!' said Eeyore proudly, stopping them outside Piglet's house. 'And the name on it, and everything!'

'Oh!' cried Christopher Robin, wondering whether to laugh or what.

'Just the house for Owl. Don't you think so, little Piglet?'

And then Piglet did a Noble Thing, and he did it in a sort of dream, while he was thinking of all the wonderful words Pooh had hummed about him.

'Yes, it's just the house for Owl,' he said grandly. 'And I hope he'll be very happy in it.' And then he gulped twice, because he had been very happy in it himself.

'What do *you* think, Christopher Robin?' asked Eeyore

a little anxiously, feeling that something wasn't quite right.

Christopher Robin had a question to ask first, and he was wondering how to ask it.

'Well,' he said at last, 'it's a very nice house, and if your own house is blown down, you *must* go somewhere else, mustn't you, Piglet? What would *you* do, if *your* house was blown down?'

Before Piglet could think, Pooh answered for him.

'He'd come and live with me,' said Pooh, 'wouldn't you, Piglet?'

Piglet squeezed his paw.

'Thank you, Pooh,' he said, 'I should love to.'

CHAPTER TEN

*in which Christopher Robin
and Pooh come to an enchanted place,
and we leave them there*

CHRISTOPHER ROBIN was going away. Nobody knew why he was going; nobody knew where he was going; indeed, nobody even knew why he knew that Christopher Robin *was* going away. But somehow or other everybody in the Forest felt that it was happening at last. Even Smallest-of-all, a friend-and-relation of Rabbit's who thought he had once seen Christopher Robin's foot, but couldn't quite be sure because perhaps it was something else, even S. of A. told himself that Things were going to be Different; and Late and Early, two other friends-and-relations, said, 'Well, Early?' and 'Well, Late?' to each other in such a hopeless sort of way that it really didn't seem any good waiting for the answer.

One day when he felt that he couldn't wait any

longer, Rabbit brained out a Notice, and this is what it said:

'Notice a meeting of everybody will meet at the House at Pooh Corner to pass a Rissolution By Order Keep to the Left Signed Rabbit.'

He had to write this out two or three times before he could get the rissolution to look like what he thought it was going to when he began to spell it; but, when at last it was finished, he took it round to everybody and read it out to them. And they all said they would come.

'Well,' said Eeyore that afternoon, when he saw them all walking up to his house, 'this *is* a surprise. Am *I* asked too?'

'Don't mind Eeyore,' whispered Rabbit to Pooh. 'I told him all about it this morning.'

Everybody said 'How-do-you-do' to Eeyore, and Eeyore said that he didn't, not to notice, and then they sat down; and as soon as they were all sitting down, Rabbit stood up again.

'We all know why we're here,' he said, 'but I have asked my friend Eeyore –'

'That's Me,' said Eeyore. 'Grand.'

'I have asked him to Propose a Rissolution.' And he sat down again. 'Now then, Eeyore,' he said.

'Don't Bustle me,' said Eeyore, getting up slowly. 'Don't now-then me.' He took a piece of paper from behind his ear, and unfolded it. 'Nobody knows anything about this,' he went on. 'This is a Surprise.' He coughed in an important way, and began again: 'What-nots and Etceteras, before I begin, or perhaps

I should say, before I end, I have a piece of Poetry to read to you. Hitherto – hitherto – a long word meaning – well, you'll see what it means directly – hitherto, as I was saying, all the Poetry in the Forest has been written by Pooh, a Bear with a Pleasing Manner but a Positively Startling Lack of Brain. The Poem which I am now about to read to you was written by Eeyore, or Myself, in a Quiet Moment. If somebody will take Roo's bull's-eye away from him, and wake up Owl, we shall all be able to enjoy it. I call it – POEM.'

This was it:

Christopher Robin is going.
At least I think he is.
Where
Nobody knows.
But he is going –
I mean he goes
(*To rhyme with 'knows'*)
Do we care?
(*To rhyme with 'where'*)
We do
Very much.
(*I haven't got a rhyme for that
    'is' in the second line yet.*
Bother.)
(*Now I haven't got a rhyme for*

bother. Bother.)
Those two bothers will have
    to rhyme with each other
Buther.
The fact is this is more difficult
    than I thought,
I ought –
(*Very good indeed*)
I ought
To begin again,
But it is easier
To stop.
Christopher Robin, good-bye,
I
(*Good*)
I
And all your friends
Sends –
I mean all your friend
Send –
(*Very awkward this, it keeps
    going wrong.*)
Well, anyhow, we send
Our love
END.

'If anybody wants to clap,' said Eeyore when he had
read this, 'now is the time to do it.'

They all clapped.

'Thank you,' said Eeyore. 'Unexpected and gratifying, if a little lacking in Smack.'

'It's much better than mine,' said Pooh admiringly, and he really thought it was.

'Well,' explained Eeyore modestly, 'it was meant to be.'

'The rissolution,' said Rabbit, 'is that we all sign it, and take it to Christopher Robin.'

So it was signed PooH, WOL, PIGLET, EOR, RABBIT, KANGA, BLOT, SMUDGE, and they all went off to Christopher Robin's house with it.

'Hallo, everybody,' said Christopher Robin – 'Hallo, Pooh.'

They all said 'Hallo,' and felt awkward and unhappy

suddenly, because it was a sort of good-bye they were saying, and they didn't want to think about it. So they stood around, and waited for somebody else to speak, and they nudged each other, and said 'Go on,' and gradually Eeyore was nudged to the front, and the others crowded behind him.

'What is it, Eeyore?' asked Christopher Robin.

Eeyore swished his tail from side to side, so as to encourage himself, and began.

'Christopher Robin,' he said, 'we've come to say – to give you – it's called – written by – but we've all – because we've heard, I mean we all know – well, you see, it's – we – you – well, that, to put it as shortly as possible, is what it is.' He turned round angrily on the others and said, 'Everybody crowds round so in this Forest. There's no Space. I never saw a more Spreading lot of animals in my life, and all in the wrong places. Can't you *see* that Christopher Robin wants to be alone? I'm going.' And he humped off.

Not quite knowing why, the others began edging away, and when Christopher Robin had finished reading POEM, and was looking up to say 'Thank you,' only Pooh was left.

'It's a comforting sort of thing to have,' said Christopher Robin, folding up the paper, and putting it in his pocket. 'Come on, Pooh,' and he walked off quickly.

'Where are we going?' said Pooh, hurrying after him,

and wondering whether it was to be an Explore or a What-shall-I-do-about-you-know-what.

'Nowhere,' said Christopher Robin.

So they began going there, and after they had walked a little way Christopher Robin said:

'What do you like doing best in the world, Pooh?'

'Well,' said Pooh, 'what I like best –' and then he had to stop and think. Because although Eating Honey *was* a very good thing to do, there was a moment just before you began to eat it which was better than when you were, but he didn't know what it was called. And then he thought that being with Christopher Robin was a very good thing to do, and having Piglet near was a very friendly thing to have; and so, when he had thought it all out, he said, 'What I like best in the whole world is Me and Piglet going to see You, and You saying, "What about a little something?" and Me saying, "Well, I shouldn't mind a little something, should you, Piglet," and it being a hummy sort of day outside, and birds singing.'

'I like that too,' said Christopher Robin, 'but what I like *doing* best is Nothing.'

'How do you do Nothing?' asked Pooh, after he had wondered for a long time.

'Well, it's when people call out at you just as you're

going off to do it, "What are you going to do, Christopher Robin?" and you say, "Oh, nothing," and then you go and do it.'

'Oh, I see,' said Pooh.

'This is a nothing sort of thing that we're doing now.'

'Oh, I see,' said Pooh again.

'It means just going along, listening to all the things you can't hear, and not bothering.'

'Oh!' said Pooh.

They walked on, thinking of This and That, and by-and-by they came to an enchanted place on the very top of the Forest called Galleons Lap, which is sixty-something trees in a circle; and Christopher Robin knew that it was enchanted because nobody had ever been able to count whether it was sixty-three or sixty-four, not even when he tied a piece of string round each tree after he had counted it. Being enchanted, its floor was not like the floor of the Forest, gorse and bracken and heather, but close-set grass, quiet and smooth and green. It was the only place in the Forest where you could sit down carelessly, without getting up again almost at once and looking for somewhere else. Sitting there they could see the whole world spread out until it reached the sky, and whatever there was all the world over was with them in Galleons Lap.

Suddenly Christopher Robin began to tell Pooh about some of the things: People called Kings and Queens and something called Factors, and a place called Europe, and an island in the middle of the sea where no ships came, and how you make a Suction Pump (if you want to), and when Knights were Knighted, and what comes from Brazil. And Pooh, his back against one of the sixty-something trees, and his paws folded in front of him, said 'Oh!' and 'I don't know,' and thought how wonderful it would be to have a Real Brain which could tell you things. And by-and-by Christopher Robin came to an end of the things, and was silent, and he sat there looking out over the world, and wishing it wouldn't stop.

But Pooh was thinking too, and he said suddenly to Christopher Robin:

'Is it a very Grand thing to be an Afternoon, what you said?'

'A what?' said Christopher Robin lazily, as he listened to something else.

'On a horse?' explained Pooh.

'A Knight?'

'Oh, was that it?' said Pooh. 'I thought it was a – Is it as Grand as a King and Factors and all the other things you said?'

'Well, it's not as grand as a King,' said Christopher Robin, and then, as Pooh seemed disappointed, he added quickly, 'but it's grander than Factors.'

'Could a Bear be one?'

'Of course he could!' said Christopher Robin. 'I'll make you one.' And he took a stick and touched Pooh on the shoulder, and said, 'Rise, Sir Pooh de Bear, most faithful of all my Knights.'

So Pooh rose and sat down and said 'Thank you,' which is the proper thing to say when you have been made a Knight, and he went into a dream again, in which he and Sir Pump and Sir Brazil and Factors lived together with a horse, and were faithful knights (all except Factors, who looked after the horse) to Good King Christopher Robin . . . and every now and then he shook his head, and said to himself, 'I'm not getting it right.' Then he began to think of all the things Christopher Robin would want to tell him when he came back from wherever he was going to, and how muddling it would be for a Bear of Very Little Brain to try and get them right in his mind. 'So, perhaps,' he said sadly to himself, 'Christopher Robin won't tell me any more,' and he wondered if being a Faithful Knight meant that you just went on being faithful without being told things.

Then, suddenly again, Christopher Robin, who was still looking at the world with his chin in his hands, called out, 'Pooh!'

'Yes?' said Pooh.

'When I'm – when – Pooh!'

'Yes, Christopher Robin?'

'I'm not going to do Nothing any more.'

'Never again?'

'Well, not so much. They don't let you.'

Pooh waited for him to go on, but he was silent again.

'Yes, Christopher Robin?' said Pooh helpfully.

'Pooh, when I'm – *you* know – when I'm *not* doing Nothing, will you come up here sometimes?'

'Just Me?'

'Yes, Pooh.'

'Will you be here too?'

'Yes, Pooh, I will be really. I *promise* I will be, Pooh.'

'That's good,' said Pooh.

'Pooh, *promise* you won't forget about me, ever. Not even when I'm a hundred.'

Pooh thought for a little.

'How old shall *I* be then?'

'Ninety-nine.'

Pooh nodded.

'I promise,' he said.

Still with his eyes on the world, Christopher Robin put out a hand and felt for Pooh's paw.

'Pooh,' said Christopher Robin earnestly, 'if I – if I'm not quite –' he stopped and tried again – 'Pooh, *whatever* happens, you *will* understand, won't you?'

'Understand what?'

'Oh, nothing.' He laughed and jumped to his feet. 'Come on!'

'Where?' said Pooh.

'Anywhere,' said Christopher Robin.

* * *

So they went off together. But wherever they go, and whatever happens to them on the way, in that enchanted place on the top of the Forest a little boy and his Bear will always be playing.